*Mariah lea[...]
the yellow r[...]
landed in Jo[...]*

Mark Hopkins stepped close to Joanna and whispered in her ear, "Well, looks like we're next."

Am I supposed to consider myself engaged? Joanna backed away to look at Mark. She knew him well enough to know that this was more than likely his idea of a proposal. She could marry Mark and live with him the rest of her life—she could give birth to a dozen little Hopkinses—and never once hear a romantic phrase from his lips. She'd loaned him one of her romance novels hoping he would get the idea of a proper courtship. He said he'd read all he could stand before he finished the first chapter, and then he laughed. "Real men don't talk like that," he'd said. Mark was about as romantic as a stick.

Now she said, "I don't know, Mark. Catching the bouquet is just a silly tradition. I don't think it means anything, really."

Then, without thinking of the consequences, she prayed, *Please, Lord, bring a dashing, romantic adventurer into my life. Send me someone exciting and unpredictable and a tad dangerous.*

M. J. CONNER is the pen name for Mildred Colvin, who is a native Missourian with three children, one son-in-law, one daughter-in-law, and three grandchildren. She and her husband spent most of their married life providing a home for foster children but now enjoy babysitting their grandchildren. Mildred writes inspirational romance because in them the truth of God's presence, even in the midst of trouble, can be portrayed. Her desire is to continue writing stories that uplift and encourage.

HEARTSONG PRESENTS

Don't miss out on any of our super romances. Write to us at the following address for information on our newest releases and club information.

Joanna's Adventure

M. J. Conner

Heartsong Presents

In memory of my sister, Jean Norval, who encouraged me to never stop writing.

A note from the Author:
I love to hear from my readers! You may correspond with me by writing:

M. J. Conner
Author Relations
PO Box 721
Uhrichsville, OH 44683

ISBN 978-1-59789-890-4

JOANNA'S ADVENTURE

All Scripture quotations are taken from the King James Version of the Bible.

All of the characters and events in this book are fictitious. Any resemblance to actual persons, living or dead, or to actual events is purely coincidental.

Our mission is to publish and distribute inspirational products offering exceptional value and biblical encouragement to the masses.

PRINTED IN THE U.S.A.

one

"I, Mariah Casey, take thee, Sherman Butler, to be my lawfully wedded husband."

Joanna Brady blinked back tears as she stood beside the bride in Cedar Bend Community Church and listened to her friend repeat the vows that joined her life to Sherman Butler, one of the richest cattle ranchers in western Kansas. At first Mariah had argued that at thirty-seven she was too old for a traditional church wedding with all the trimmings. Joanna and Carrie Nolan, Sherman's married daughter, finally persuaded her otherwise. Joanna smiled through her tears, glad that Mariah had agreed at last. She looked radiant in white satin.

"Are we married yet?" asked Hope, Mariah's young daughter who sat between Lucas and Carrie Nolan in the front pew, her voice carrying across the church.

Carrie put a finger across the four-year-old's lips and shook her head. "Not yet," she whispered.

Hope squirmed in the seat before she sighed deeply. Joanna suppressed a giggle. In the few short months Hope had lived with Mariah, she had changed from a mute, frightened little girl into an exuberant, headstrong chatterbox. Joanna could not imagine what had moved Felicia Wainwright to give her

5

unwanted orphaned niece to Cedar Bend's schoolteacher, but she thanked God every day that she had done so. Mariah and Hope were destined to be together just as Sherman and Mariah were meant for each other.

"I will love, honor, and obey you as long as we both shall live."

Mark Hopkins, sitting across the church from the Nolans, caught Joanna's gaze and smiled. She returned his smile, hoping he didn't read more into it than she intended. She loved Mark. Had for as long as she could remember. But she was not in love with him. He was comfortable to be with. There were no surprises with Mark. No excitement. No romance. He bore no resemblance to the heroes in the romance novels she read. Mark was too predictable for that. Joanna's entire life had been comfortable and predictable. And boring. Like a parched flower thirsting for water, Joanna craved excitement and romance.

"Sherman, you may kiss your bride."

Joanna watched as Mr. Butler lifted the veil from Mariah's beaming face and kissed her with love and reverence. Joanna sighed while time rolled backward in her mind.

Seven years ago, at thirteen, Joanna hadn't thought much about boys—until Clay Shepherd walked into the one-room schoolhouse and took a seat in the last row. Like most of the girls in eighth grade, Joanna couldn't help noticing the older boy's dark good looks.

With glistening black hair and olive skin setting off his pale blue eyes, he had only to lift the corners of his mouth and the girls fell over themselves trying to get his attention. Except for Carrie Butler. She said he had a wild streak a mile wide.

Joanna didn't listen to Carrie. Oh, she didn't follow Clay around like some of the girls, but she spent a fair share of time daydreaming, fitting him into the plot of her life as her hero. He did odd jobs for her doctor father and listened politely when her mother talked to him, giving motherly advice, so she saw him often, yet he never paid much attention to her. That's probably why he took her by surprise at the Christmas play rehearsal.

She still remembered arriving early at the schoolhouse only to find no one there yet. She started to leave when Clay stepped through the door. His quick grin when his gaze darted to the mistletoe hanging above her head then back to her face had her heart pounding. Before she fully understood his intentions, he grabbed her upper arms and pulled her toward him. His grin disappeared as he closed the remaining few inches to place a kiss on her upturned lips.

He'd laughed then and said, "That's what you get, Joanna, for standing under the mistletoe."

She had been so shocked she could only stare at him in silence. But she had never forgotten her one and only kiss.

"Are we married now, Carrie?" Hope's loud whisper brought Joanna back to the present. She turned to look at the little girl.

"Yes." Carrie kissed Hope's rosy cheek. "We are married, little sister."

ð

An hour and a half later in the back room of the Cattleman's Association Hall, Carrie and Joanna helped Mariah change into a buttercup-colored suit.

"I probably should have chosen a more conservative color," Mariah fretted. "The stagecoach is so dusty."

"Not this time of year," Carrie reassured her.

"With last night's rain you shouldn't have a thing to worry about." Joanna set a small matching yellow hat atop Mariah's elaborately arranged ebony curls. "You are a beautiful bride, Mariah."

"Thank you." Mariah's cheeks flushed a becoming pink. "Carrie, are you sure you'll be all right with Hope?"

"We'll be fine." Carrie hugged her new stepmother. "Don't you waste one minute of your wedding trip worrying about Hope. I always wanted a sister. We are going to have so much fun."

"Oh dear." Mariah pulled on snug-fitting white gloves. "I feel as though I'm being pulled in two directions. I want to go. And I want to stay. Do I look presentable?"

"You look beautiful." Carrie laughed. "Please don't take offense, but the first time I saw you, I never imagined you could be so. . .so. . .human."

"I was a real old maid, wasn't I?"

"You certainly were." Carrie stretched up to kiss the taller woman's cheek. "I love you, Mother."

"Oh, Carrie." Tears rimmed Mariah's blue eyes as she hugged the younger woman. "I love you, too."

Joanna brushed away her own tears. "We'd better go before we all start blubbering." She thrust into the bride's hand the bouquet of yellow roses Mariah had carried down the aisle. "Don't forget you are supposed to throw these."

"Joanna, my dear friend." Mariah brushed a final tear from Joanna's cheek. "A true friend is a gift of God. When I arrived here last year, I knew no one except my cousins. You were the first to become my friend, and I thank God every day for the gift of your friendship."

"And I thank Him for bringing you to Cedar Bend. My life has been greatly enriched by knowing you, Mariah. Now, we must go. Your husband is waiting for you."

"So he is." Mariah opened the white-beaded handbag she carried. "I have something for you, Joanna. This is a gift from Sherman and me." She pressed a paper into Joanna's hand. "It's the deed to my house. I have removed everything I want to keep. The rest is yours for the library."

"I can't take this." Joanna looked at the deed in her hand. "It's too much."

"Nonsense. Sell it and use the money to build your library. Or turn your house into a library. It's an ideal location."

"Not *my* library." Joanna shook her head. "It's *our* library."

"It will be Cedar Bend's library." Mariah leaned down to kiss her young friend's cheek. "I love you, Joanna."

&

Later, Mariah and Sherman ran to catch the stagecoach through a hail of rice. They waved out the window as the stagecoach pulled away.

"Mariah!" Gladys Jacobs's voice rose above the cheers of the assembled townsfolk. "Throw your bouquet."

Mariah leaned farther out the window and tossed the yellow roses. They arched through the air and landed in Joanna's outstretched hands.

Mark Hopkins stepped close to Joanna and whispered in her ear, "Well, looks like we're next."

Am I supposed to consider myself engaged? Joanna backed away to look at Mark. She knew him well enough to know that this was more than likely his idea of a proposal. She could marry Mark and live with him the rest of her life—she could give birth to a dozen little Hopkinses—and never once hear a romantic phrase from his lips. She'd loaned him one of her romance novels hoping he would get the idea of a proper courtship. He said he'd read all he could stand before he finished the first chapter, and then he laughed. "Real men don't talk like that," he'd said. Mark was about as romantic as a stick.

Now she said, "I don't know, Mark. Catching the bouquet is just a silly tradition. I don't think it means anything, really."

Then, without thinking of the consequences, she prayed, *Please, Lord, bring a dashing, romantic adventurer into my life. Send me someone exciting and unpredictable and a tad dangerous.*

two

Western Nebraska, a few days later

Clay Shepherd knew when he signed on as a wrangler at the Crooked S that they were a rough bunch. After he had been there less than a week, he noticed most of the cows had altered brands. A bit of rustling didn't bother Clay—long as someone else did the rustling—but he for sure wanted nothing to do with robbing a bank.

"Count me out," he said when Bob Simms approached him with the ill-conceived scheme. "I don't want any part of it."

"I thought you was game." Simms scowled. "You a yellow belly, Shepherd?"

"I'm no coward," Clay retorted. "But I'm not a fool, either. Robbing a government payroll in broad daylight will buy you a place on Boot Hill."

"I ain't aimin' to get shot." Simms's hand strayed to the gun tied low on his right hip. "Neither is the rest of the boys."

"If you're dead set on doing this, why don't you do it after dark when nobody's around?"

"Wouldn't work. That payroll will only be there one night. The way I figure it, they'll have guards posted. We'll hit 'em around noon when they ain't expectin' us."

Simms was shy a few marbles, although Clay couldn't say that to his face. The town would be teeming with cavalry.

Not to mention the sheriff and his deputies. The Crooked S gang would be lucky to escape the bank alive. Clay had no intention of dying just yet, but with the way Simms eyed him while toying with his six-shooter, Clay figured he'd be a dead man right quick if he refused to ride with them. That little fact didn't give him a whole lot of choice.

"Sounds as though you've come up with a brilliant plan," he finally said. "Count me in."

A grimace that passed for a grin crossed Simms's thick face while his hand moved from the stock of his pistol. The two men shook hands. "Glad you decided to join us, Shepherd. You understand, bein' as how you're new and all, I can only give you ten percent of the take. Me and the other two boys will divvy up the rest. That agreeable to you?"

Clay noticed Simms's burly hand hovering around the stock of his gun again. "Sounds more than generous to me," he agreed.

"Good!" Simms started away then turned back. "By the way, I can't let you go in the bank with us, neither. Your job will be to hold the horses in the alley behind the bank. You agreeable to that?"

"Yes sir, Mr. Simms. It will probably be for the best. Seeing as how I have never robbed a bank before."

Clay grinned as he watched Simms walk away. He had no intention of getting himself killed. Escaping Simms and his gang was going to be easier than he first imagined. While they were in the bank—most likely getting themselves blown to kingdom come—he'd be lighting a shuck out of town.

Texas. I haven't been in Texas for a while. I'll head south. In case any of the Simms gang survives, they'll never find me there.

Clay whistled as he headed for the bunkhouse.

❧

Almost a week later the sun beat down on the men's heads and shoulders as they rode to town with a cloud of dust rising behind them. Simms passed a bottle around, and all the men except Clay took a hefty swig. When his turn came, he lifted the bottle to his lips but only pretended to drink. By the time they rode into town, Clay was the only clearheaded member of the gang.

They split up just outside town, going in by twos so they wouldn't attract attention. Simms stayed with Clay. As they ambled down the main street of town, Clay noticed the sheriff leaning against a storefront across from the bank. A guard stood outside the bank's door.

He pointed out the two men to Simms, certain there were more he hadn't seen. "Sure you want to go through with this?"

"You ain't gettin' lily-livered, are ya?" Simms sneered.

"Nope." Clay figured he'd better not push the issue. "Just thought you might have changed your mind."

"Not a chance."

They took their time riding through town then doubled back to the bank at high noon where they met the other two gang members.

"You wait fer us here, Shepherd," Simms said as soon as they were in place behind the bank.

The men dismounted and handed Clay the reins to their horses. "Soon as you hear the signal, you ride 'round front with our horses like I told you."

"Yes sir, Mr. Simms, I'll do that," Clay said. "What was that signal again, just so's I don't forget?"

"One shot." The husky outlaw stumbled. "I reckon I oughta not have let you share our bottle. Can't even remember a simple signal. Come on, boys. Let's go."

Clay watched the three men slip around the corner of the brick building. One of them tugged his bandanna into place. They would be lucky if they even got inside the bank before they were shot.

Clay dropped the lines to the three horses entrusted to his care and slapped the nearest horse across the hindquarters. The horse ran a few paces away before stopping to take a bite of tall grass by the side of the alley. The other horses milled around, then bolted at the sound of yelling and gunfire. Clay swung into the saddle and patted his stallion on the neck. "Reckon that's our signal, Lucky?"

A volley of gunshots rang out. Clay winced and nodded. "Yep, that must be it."

He kneed his mount, and they rode slowly out of town in the opposite direction from the way they had entered.

❧

Two days later Clay crossed into western Kansas heading south. The air had been heavy laden with humidity all day. Now, as late evening approached, the sky became a green-tinged yellow bruise. Nothing stirred, and that fact concerned Clay as much as anything.

"There's a twister coming for sure." Clay patted the black stallion's gleaming neck. "We'd better find shelter, Lucky, if we don't want to get blown back to Nebraska."

They had been following a winding creek. Clay dismounted and led Lucky down a shallow embankment to the water's edge. After both man and beast had drunk their fill of the clear, tepid water, Clay turned to leave, spotting a rock overhang facing east. He led the stallion to the shelter nature had carved high in the creek bank. Deep enough to be a cave and well out of the water, it provided the protection he and Lucky needed.

Clay removed his saddle and rubbed Lucky down before laying out his bedroll. He built a small fire in the mouth of the cave and settled back on his bed just as the wind picked up. The tongues of his campfire danced to the whining tune of the wind, but most of the moist air rushed past his hideout, making Clay glad he had sought shelter when he did. Rain splattered at first then came down in torrents as the shrieking wind turned into a deafening roar. Within twenty minutes the rain stopped, the wind died down, and the black sky filled with twinkling pinpoints of light.

Clay stood and stroked the black stallion's muzzle. "Well, Lucky, looks like we missed the worst of it."

He gave the horse one final pat before crawling onto his bedroll. In minutes he fell asleep.

๏

Clay headed out the next morning at daybreak. He saw evidence of the storm all around, in the flattened grass that had reached Lucky's underbelly the day before. Near midmorning he came upon some scraps of milled lumber. Not far beyond, he saw the battered homestead. A large tree in the backyard had been pulled from the ground, its branches chewed to stubs then dropped on the roof of the house. His first instinct was to ride on by when he saw no evidence of life. After all, he reasoned that anyone in what remained of the small cabin would be either dead or close to it. Still, someone might need help, and if not, there might be something worth salvaging among the wreckage.

He rode up to the homesite and dismounted beside the destroyed cabin. The roof had caved in with the weight of the old oak tree, but the front two rooms seemed to have escaped serious damage. Clay entered to shuffle his way through the debris left from the storm.

He called out, "Hey, anybody here?" He listened and heard nothing, so he began sifting through the mess, looking for anything of value. When he opened a cabinet door, he heard a faint sound coming from the rubble at the back of the house.

He lifted his head and listened. There it was again. Sounded like a kitten. He'd always been a sucker for the helpless, so he turned toward the mewing sound. Probably the little thing had gotten caught in a corner and couldn't find its way out. He pushed aside enough debris to enter the bedroom then stopped short. A heavy beam had fallen across the walnut bedstead. The man and woman sleeping there never had a chance. He bowed his head in a moment of respect.

Again he heard the mew of the kitten. A few feet from the bed a door had fallen across what looked like a cradle. The mewing sounds seemed to come from there.

Clay lifted the door and tossed it to one side. "What in the world—" He stood looking at the red-faced occupant of the cradle. The baby's eyes were squeezed shut with its mouth wide open, exposing toothless gums. The mewing he'd heard before sounded full force, like that of a squalling infant now.

"You are one ugly little person," Clay said over the annoying sound.

The baby hushed in midshriek. Little eyes opened and regarded Clay with a light blue gaze.

"What's the matter, buddy? Are you hungry?" Kitten or baby, Clay couldn't walk away.

A crock in the kitchen, sitting untouched on the sideboard, held milk. Clay rummaged through the debris until he gave up finding a bottle with a nipple to feed the infant. When the baby's cries finally seemed to be growing weak, he decided to try spoon-feeding. He'd done it with a kitten, so why not with a human baby? After a few tries with the baby still in the crib, he decided he'd have to find a place to sit and hold the little guy so the milk would go down better.

He brushed dust and pieces of the ceiling from a kitchen chair then carried the baby wrapped in a blanket into the next room. By holding him in a reclining position, Clay found he was able to get a steady supply of milk down.

"Is your tummy full now?" Clay asked when the baby seemed to lose interest. "I sure hope so."

He carried the baby into the bedroom and put him back in the crib.

"What am I supposed to do with you?" He stood looking down at the wriggling tyke while considering his options. He could walk away. Leave him here. Probably wouldn't take a kid this size long to starve.

The baby looked up at him with a wide-eyed stare, almost as if he expected him to solve his problems. "Sorry, kid. You can't go with me. I travel alone."

A soft sigh lifted the baby's chest.

"I know, kid. It's a tough world. Your ma and pa are both dead. My ma died when I wasn't much older than you. Of course I had Pa. He's dead now, too."

The baby's eyelids appeared to be too heavy to remain open. "Reckon that makes us both orphans."

Clay watched the baby fight against sleep and felt a kinship with the little one. He couldn't walk away knowing a death sentence awaited this innocent little one. What he needed was a mother. Someone to care, like Mrs. Brady had cared for him long ago when he was an unlovable teen. A slow grin crossed his face.

"You know, kid, I just had an idea. We can't be much more than a day's ride from Cedar Bend." Clay studied the sleeping infant's face. The kid wasn't so hard on the eyes when he wasn't screaming. "There's a woman in Cedar Bend who would take real good care of you. She's a doctor's wife, so you'd be in good hands. I'll take you to her."

Clay foraged around in the kitchen until he found a covered tin container. He filled it with milk, hoping it was fresh from the night before and would keep a day or two. He put it in his saddlebag along with some cans of beans for himself and went back for the baby. The kid's diaper hung halfway to his knees, heavy and wet. Clay removed the diaper and confirmed the baby was a boy. He held the baby's kicking feet out of the way and put on a clean diaper. He didn't do much of a job pinning on the replacement, but he reckoned it would hold until they got to Mrs. Brady.

After digging one large grave, he buried the man and woman, saying as much as he could remember of Psalm 23. Funny, he hadn't thought of any scripture verses in years. Not since he left Cedar Bend and the woman who'd been as much a mother to him as he'd ever had. He hadn't thought of the Bradys in a long time, but he knew without a doubt they would welcome the orphaned baby just as they'd welcomed him when he needed their friendship.

He took baby clothes, blankets, whatever he could find that looked like it belonged to the little guy, and stuffed it all in his saddlebags. A few more canned goods went in after that. He found a family Bible with names inside and decided the kid would like to have it when he was older. Then he tied half a bedsheet around his neck, devising a sling to carry the baby. He mounted Lucky with one hand holding the baby against his chest and headed south.

three

Joanna set a platter of sausage, eggs, and oatmeal on the table in front of her father and a bowl of oatmeal across the table for herself. She bowed her head while her father prayed then picked up her spoon and dipped it into the oatmeal sitting in front of her. That with a glass of milk made up a satisfying breakfast for her now.

Her friendship with Mariah Casey had given Joanna more than just someone to talk to. Although seventeen years apart in age, the two women had grown close soon after Mariah moved to Cedar Bend. They both had nursed their mothers through sickness and grown up with little time for friendships. They found they had much in common in spite of the years separating them. Joanna also found she had lost some weight and felt better after following Mariah's example of eating fewer sweets.

"When are Sherm and his new wife due back home?" Dr. Brady asked.

"In the next few days, I suppose." Joanna took a sip of milk. "They've been gone almost two weeks already. Carrie said she got a card from them just yesterday, and all it said was they were having a wonderful time."

Joanna giggled. "I don't think Carrie quite knows what to make of her father off on a honeymoon. She's being a good sport about it, though."

"She'll do fine." Dr. Brady loaded his fork with egg then stabbed a small piece of sausage. "So what are your plans for the day?"

Joanna watched him slip his fork into his mouth and felt no desire for the greasy food she had once craved. If her mother were still alive, she knew she would be so proud of her accomplishment in controlling her appetite. Sometimes she missed her mother with an almost physical pain, even after two years. "I'm going to have a good look at Mariah's old house. I still can't believe she gave it to me. Well, actually to the town. I want to see what needs to be done to turn it into a library."

"Sounds like a worthwhile project." Her father nodded and took a drink of milk.

"Oh, it is." Joanna felt the inner glow that always warmed her at the thought of the library that would soon become a reality. "I'm sure as word spreads others will want to become involved as well."

Dr. Brady wiped his hands on his napkin and smiled. "While you are at the library, I shall be making my rounds. Mr. Hartley is my first stop, and the Danville boy is due to have his cast taken off."

"How is Mr. Hartley doing with his skin condition?" Joanna stood and began gathering dishes. She cleaned the kitchen while her father filled her in on the health of his patients.

Several minutes later, with a ray of sunlight peeking from behind a cloud, Joanna secured her bonnet and waved to her father as he set off in his buggy. She closed the kitchen door and headed on foot toward town, being careful to skirt mud puddles left from the overnight rain they had received. The air smelled fresh and clean after the rain. Droplets of water still clung to leaves, creating an occasional shower when she walked underneath.

She and her father lived at the edge of town. Behind their house the prairie spread all the way to the horizon on gently rolling hills, while their front yard faced the dirt road that led past the Cattleman's Association Hall to a handful of stores, two churches, and a one-room schoolhouse. Mariah's house sat on Main Street, an easy walk from the cluster of buildings that made up the business district of Cedar Bend.

But it was Mariah's house no longer. Joanna felt the thrill of her dream soon becoming reality. Before too many days passed, the entire town would think of the little bungalow as their library. She smiled as she set a brisk pace down the side of the street, waving and speaking briefly to those she met.

She slowed when she neared Conway's Feed Store at the corner of Main and Pine streets. Mark Hopkins had started working for Jack Conway as soon as he entered his teens. She searched for a glimpse of him when she came abreast of the old whiteboard building and then hurried past. As much as she cared for Mark, she didn't feel like talking to him today. He'd been trying to get her to go on an outing with him for the last two weeks, and she couldn't say yes with a thankful heart. But today Mark was nowhere in sight, so Joanna again set a steady pace.

Two blocks later, she opened the gate to Mariah's house and started up the walk, stopping after several steps to look at the small house that belonged to her now. Flowers stood in a stately row on either side of the walk to the front porch.

So much like Mariah. Joanna smiled as she thought of the woman who had become her best friend. She'd be glad when the Butlers returned from their trip. Always efficient, Mariah would be a great help with the library. If she wasn't too busy with her new family, that was.

Joanna crossed the porch and pushed the front door open. Except for the few special pieces taken to her new home, Mariah had left her furniture to be used in the library. Joanna looked around the front room as her imagination placed a desk near the door. The librarian would need to be handy to greet patrons and check books as they went out and came back. Shelves could be built in each room, maybe three or four freestanding with the ends secured to one wall. That would leave room for a couch in the corner opposite the desk so people could sit and read at their leisure.

Giving a little twirl in the center of the room, Joanna smiled in satisfaction. She could just see Cedar Bend folk pouring into her library. Their library. A place of learning and culture and dreams set free.

A sharp knock at the door brought Joanna back to earth. She turned as Carrie Nolan poked her head inside. Gleaming auburn hair framed her pretty face and wide smile. "Are we open for business yet?"

Joanna laughed while her friend stepped inside followed by Hope. The child ran across the room to give Joanna a hug. "I love you, Aunt Joanna."

Returning the little girl's hug, Joanna felt a rush of warmth fill her heart. Hope always brightened her world.

"I love you too, Hope."

"My mama's coming home." Hope stepped back and looked

at Joanna with wide, serious eyes. "We not leaving my new daddy's house, though, so you can have this old house. Him told me we gonna stay forever and forever."

"My, that's a long time." Joanna stood and shared a smile with her friend while Carrie's little stepsister explained that forever meant as long as Mama, Papa, and she should live.

Carrie said, "We were on our way to town and saw the door open. Are you getting ready to start work on the library?"

"Oh, I wish I could." Joanna sighed as she glanced around the room again. "It will take a while to get this place in shape. We need shelves and the right furnishings. I'd like to have an area rug in each room and different curtains at the windows. We have to buy books—lots of books."

"You are right." Carrie tapped a slender finger against her lower lip as she studied the room. "What we need is some way to raise money. And not just to get the library itself ready. There needs to be money on an ongoing basis. What about a salary for the librarian? And don't forget the expenses."

Joanna turned toward the wood-burning stove in the corner and groaned. "Oh no, I never even thought about that. There's a pump for water in the kitchen, but if I can't find a donor for wood, I'll have to buy some, at least in the winter."

"Will you leave the kitchen as it is?" Carrie stepped across the floor to peer through the open doorway into the next room. As Hope ran past, Carrie rested her hand across her flat stomach in an unconscious gesture of protection toward her unborn child.

Joanna joined Carrie and watched Hope circle the oak table that took up the center of the room. She smiled at the little girl's antics as Hope climbed into one chair after another.

Carrie called to her, "Hope, be careful. I don't want you getting hurt."

"I not get hurt, Carrie." Hope stretched to reach a chair set back from the others, gave a little hop, and landed safely on it.

Joanna giggled when she heard Carrie's breath rush out. "She'll be all right."

Carrie and Joanna moved back into the living room while Hope continued playing on the chairs. "I'd just hate for Mariah to come home and find bruises on her daughter."

A burst of laughter from Joanna brought a smile to Carrie's lips before she, too, laughed and said, "This has been an experience for Luke and me. I think I have a better idea of what being a mother will be like."

"I heard about a man who married late in life." Joanna leaned against the door frame to tell her story. "When their first baby was born and then started crawling, he took every bit of furniture that was not padded out of the house. That child grew up afraid to play games with the other children because she feared getting hurt. Any new experience was something to be dreaded. She missed so much of life because of too much fear."

"How terrible," Carrie said.

"Yes, I think so." Joanna looked out through the front window as if she could see beyond the small Kansas town set in the middle of the prairie. "I want some excitement in my life. I've never told anyone this before, but I'd love to have an exciting adventure. Do something daring for a change." She grinned as she brought her gaze back to Carrie. "Maybe something just a tad dangerous so I could tell my children and grandchildren about my adventures someday."

"I don't know, Joanna." Carrie shook her head. "Our foreman, Cyrus, always says you should be careful what you wish for because you just might get it."

"Then I shall wish for excitement and pray for it, too." Joanna giggled. "Actually, I already have been."

Carrie looked beyond Joanna through the open door leading outside. "Does Mark Hopkins have anything to do with the answer to your prayers?"

"Mark Hopkins! Why would you think. . . ?" Joanna's voice trailed off as she realized Carrie was looking at something. She turned just as she heard the first footstep on the wooden porch.

Mark lifted a hand to knock. What was the use in hiding from him? She couldn't avoid him forever, and she really did like Mark. As a friend. If only he didn't want more. If only her knight in shining armor would ride into town and sweep her off her feet.

"Good morning, Mark," Joanna called out before he could knock. "Come on in."

"I saw you go by the feed store." He smiled. "Figured you might be headed this way."

"Carrie and I have been discussing ways to raise money for the library." Joanna turned away from Mark. "Carrie, I never did answer your question about the kitchen. I really don't know. I guess we could leave it as a kitchen in case it's needed, at least until we need the room for more books. What do you think?"

Carrie's curious glance from Mark to Joanna said she thought there might be more under the surface than Joanna wanted to admit. But she kept her counsel on that subject. "It never hurts to build gradually. We could have a box supper to raise money. And we could ask for book donations. Maybe folks around town would be willing to share any books they might have."

"Those are wonderful ideas, Carrie." Joanna, feeling guilty for excluding Mark, turned to face him. "Don't you agree, Mark?"

He shrugged. "I came by to tell you that I'll pick you up for the church social at six o'clock Saturday night."

How typical of Mark. Joanna couldn't remember him inviting her to attend the social with him. Instead, he just assumed they would go together.

She started to tell him just what she thought of his assumptions when a small streak rushed past her skirt.

"Mark!" Hope launched herself into Mark's arms. He lifted the little girl above his head and gave her a little toss. Her delighted squeals brightened Joanna's mood, and she again saw Mark for who he was—a good man with good intentions. So what if he took her for granted? He was solid and reliable. Shouldn't those be the traits she looked for in a husband? Who needed exciting and unpredictable? Who needed romance? She did, but she wasn't likely to get what she needed, so she might as well take what she had.

As Mark set Hope back on the floor, Joanna forced a smile. "All right, Mark. I'll be ready at six."

He gave her a quick nod. "I'll walk you home."

Carrie took Hope's hand and stepped toward the door. "We do need to get to town before Luke comes looking for us. He's taking us to the hotel dining room for lunch. We'll get together again, Joanna, to discuss our ideas for the library."

"Yes, that will be good." Joanna watched her friends go down the walk and turned to Mark. "Would you like to look around and see what I'm planning?"

She took his shrug as agreement and began explaining what she would like to do with the living room. As they went through the house, Mark had little to say but seemed determined to stay until she finished. Finally, she said, "All right, Mark, I'm ready to go."

Mark crossed the road before setting off at a brisk pace, and Joanna fell into step beside him.

Their conversation consisted of Mark's work and the house he planned to begin building soon. Joanna tried to steer away from talking about his house, because she knew he intended for her to live there with him one day. But each attempt at bringing the library to the front was ignored until Joanna gave up.

"I've been storing materials in my dad's barn," Mark said as they stepped off the boardwalk.

Joanna stopped. Mark plowed ahead through the muddy road, leaving a good impression of his boot soles with each step. She looked around and realized they were on the opposite side of the street from the way she had come earlier. That's how she had missed the mud before.

As she tried to decide what to do, Mark stopped on the other side of the road and looked at her. "Aren't you coming?"

Clenching her teeth in frustration, Joanna wondered if he were blind. How could he not know that a woman's shoes were not as sturdy or waterproof as his boots? She lifted her skirts just enough to keep them from dragging in the mud and picked her way carefully around the huge puddle until she had crossed the road.

Mark took her arm when she reached his side and helped her step on the boardwalk, as if that made up for not helping before. She felt like jerking her arm away but didn't.

"I guess we could have gone a different way," he said. "I didn't think about the mud being a problem."

"It's all right, Mark. I'm across now."

What difference did it make? Mark would never change.

Lord, I don't even want to change Mark. He doesn't need changing. He just needs someone more suited to him. But what about me, God? Isn't there someone out there who can see past the end of his nose? Don't you have someone You can send that will be gallant, ready to step between me and danger? Even if it is just mud. Please, Lord. Send me someone who will set my heart racing.

four

Clay figured on making good time. He'd never ridden with a baby strapped to his chest before, but it wasn't too bad. They'd already gone several miles. The kid bounced a lot, which was fine with Clay as long as he kept quiet. Kids liked that rocking motion, didn't they? Yep, he was doing just fine.

He had no sooner congratulated himself when a funny gurgling noise came from the baby. He looked down as a spray of what looked like clabbered milk shot from the kid's mouth. In the next instant, a squall that nearly burst Clay's eardrums sounded. At least the kid had a good set of lungs.

That high-pitched wail was the most annoying sound he'd ever heard. When Lucky faltered, Clay figured he'd better do something fast before his horse had a nervous fit and hurt them all.

"Whoa," he said to Lucky. "Reckon we'd better take a breather."

He swung from the saddle and wrinkled his nose. A breather was definitely in order. Soured milk and something else accosted his nostrils. Something that reminded him of an outhouse.

"Yuck." Clay lifted the crying baby from the sling and held him out at arms' length. "What I wouldn't give for a woman right about now."

He looked around the grass-covered prairie, but no woman

materialized. He could see clear to the horizon in all directions, so he didn't figure one would come walking up anytime soon. Only a broken-down cabin broke the view. Looked like he was on his own, and at the moment that didn't sit so well.

"Should have left you back there in that cabin when I thought you was a kitten." Blue eyes looked across at him trustingly. Misplaced trust, but at least the kid had stopped crying.

"You know, I'd much rather wrestle a wild bear than mess with you." The baby regarded him with a solemn expression.

When Clay looked around for a place to lay the kid, his gaze hit the front of his duster where a stream of clabbered milk clung. "Hey, what'd you have to go and do that for?"

Figuring his duster had already gotten the worst of the milk attack, he held the baby in one arm and shrugged out of the opposite sleeve. Shifting sides, he let his duster fall to the ground. Laying the baby on it, he rummaged through his saddlebag for a fresh diaper and gown. Using drinking water and another diaper, he swiped most of the milk from his duster first and the baby next. He stepped back and looked down at the little one. His face scrunched and his mouth puckered just before the squalling started again.

"Hey, stop that. I know I ain't finished the job. But give a little slack here. You're my first. Got any hints on this thing?" He held the clean diaper up and looked it over. The one he'd changed at the cabin had been folded. This one just looked like a square piece of cloth to him. He looked at the dirty, soaked diaper still on the baby. The thing was bunched up between the kid's legs. He looked back at the cloth in his hand and wondered why they didn't come formfitting like trousers. No man should have to tackle a job like this.

He knelt again by the baby and touched one finger to the pin holding the diaper in place. A rumble of thunder sounded in the southwest. Clay looked up. Clouds were rolling in. They needed to take shelter and hope another tornado didn't blow through the area.

In a hurry now, Clay unhooked the pin and pulled the diaper back. He gagged at the contents but used the dirty diaper to wipe most of the grime from the baby. After several attempts to make a triangle, he folded the clean diaper into a rectangle and hoped it would fit. It didn't, but it would have to do. He tugged it together in front and pinned it.

"You sag here and there, and I don't reckon a woman would have done it this way, but you'll do until next time." Clay just hoped there wouldn't be many next times until he reached Cedar Bend. He slipped the gown over the baby's head, glad it was roomy enough to move around when the kid held fists up by his shoulders and wouldn't give.

Clay worked the sleeves on anyway, amazed at how hard dressing an infant was. "You're a lot stronger than I thought you'd be. Shame you'll probably grow up to be a doctor like Doc Brady. With those muscles, you could wrangle horses with the best of 'em."

Joanna Brady's face appeared in Clay's mind. "Reckon you'll have a big sister. She'll know how to take care of you a lot better than I do."

He grinned, remembering the day he'd surprised her under the mistletoe. He'd taken a kiss, too. He knew now it hadn't been much of a kiss, but he hadn't forgotten it—or her. He couldn't help wondering if he'd see her when he got to town.

Naw, she wouldn't want to see the likes of him. He'd just drop the baby off and run. She was probably married with a kid of her own by now, anyhow.

A splat of water hit his duster. He didn't bother checking the sky. He didn't figure he had time. Settling the baby back in his sling, Clay grabbed his duster, threw it on, and swung into the saddle. Turning Lucky's nose toward the dilapidated cabin he'd seen in the distance, he hoped they could reach it in time.

A few minutes later, Clay slid from the horse and, holding his duster over the baby, ran to the house through a pelting rain. He banged on the door and listened, keeping his shoulder hunched to shield the baby. Only the drumming sound of rain against the roof answered. Hoping he didn't startle any varmints of the four-legged kind, or two-legged for that matter, he pulled his six-shooter from the holster on his hip and shoved the door open.

The heavy oak door swung back with enough force to hit the wall. Something small and gray darted behind a cupboard in the corner. Clay scanned the one room before stepping inside. He shoved his gun back in place as he let his muscles relax. The *plink* of water hitting the wooden table before splattering onto the floor sounded loud in the otherwise quiet room. A musty smell greeted him. Clay looked up at the dripping ceiling.

"Hey, buddy, what do you say? Think this place will do?" When the kid didn't answer, Clay said, "Come on now. It's not that bad. Just one leak if you don't count the broken window. And there's a bed in the corner. Which side do you want?"

Clay figured he'd better shake out the bedcovers before laying the kid down. Wouldn't do to find something alive hiding in their bed. From what he could see in the dim room, the table looked like the cleanest place. He swiped his finger through thick dust on the dry end and shrugged. At least it had been wiped off once, even if not lately.

"Hey, a little dirt never hurt anyone, did it, buddy?" He slipped the sling off and laid the baby on the table. The little guy looked at him as if trying to understand this new experience. "Tell you what. You stay right there and don't move. I have to get the saddlebags and take care of Lucky. You do that and I'll get you some more milk. Okay?"

When the baby didn't cry, Clay figured that meant he'd better get a move on. He just hoped the kid didn't decide to scoot over or roll off the table. For a guy so little, three feet or so would be a long way to fall.

Clay ran from the cabin to his horse. He led Lucky up the one step to the porch and tied him to a corner post. If the wind didn't blow too hard, Lucky should have shelter there and still be able to reach the tall grass growing against the cabin. Clay patted the horse's neck and rubbed his long, sleek nose. Although his duster took the brunt of the rain blowing under the porch roof, a shiver moved across his shoulders. He unhooked the saddlebags and lifted them from the horse. When he tossed them inside the door, he checked on the baby and saw two little fists flailing in the air. At least he hadn't moved. And he was quiet. Couldn't ask for more than that.

Clay's stomach rumbled. Since he was hungry, it was a pretty safe bet the kid would be, too. And that meant he might start crying at any time. The thought of listening to any more of those ear-piercing cries had Clay moving faster than usual. Finished outside, he closed the door against the rain.

Ignoring his own stomach, Clay opened the container of milk and set it on the table. He pulled an old wooden rocker from the wall and settled in it with the baby. While the kid swallowed each spoonful of milk, Clay set the rocker into motion. He'd sure hate for one of his cowboy buddies to see him rocking a baby, but to tell the truth, he didn't mind the doing of it one bit.

After a while, the infant started wheezing, like he couldn't breathe right. He kept taking the milk as if nothing was wrong, but Clay didn't like that sound at all. A couple more spoonfuls and he decided something must be caught in the kid's throat. His heart pounding with fear for the little one's safety, Clay slung him over his shoulder. He pounded the little guy's back, hoping to dislodge whatever blocked his airway. After three or four firm, open-hand swats in the middle of the tiny back, a belch that would have done any cowboy proud sounded in Clay's ear.

He pulled the baby back and looked at him. His breathing sounded fine, but his face scrunched up just like it always did before he cried. Clay tucked him back in the crook of his arm and poured another bit of milk into his mouth before he could let out a sound. He didn't wheeze anymore, and he didn't cry after he finished eating. Instead, his eyes drifted shut and he went to sleep. That's when Clay felt something warm and wet spread over his lap.

Later, in the darkest part of the night, Clay dreamed he had just lassoed a young steer. He threw him to the ground, dust rising in a choking cloud as he tied the short rope around the calf's feet. He smelled sweat and—outhouse? The calf looked up at him with a baby's light blue eyes and puckered his mouth just before he bawled. Clay sat up, confused when the calf's bawling turned into the baby's cries.

He rubbed his eyes and looked toward the bed next to the wall. Buddy lay on his back. Both little fists and two little feet fought the air where the covers had been. Red-faced and squalling at the top of his lungs, the baby demanded attention.

Clay gained a new respect for the female gender as he changed the fourth diaper in less than ten hours. He couldn't wait to get to Cedar Bend and would have headed out right then except the rain still beat a steady tattoo against the tin roof.

With a clean diaper more or less covering his roommate, Clay thought his job was done. But the kid kept crying, arching his back as if he were having a mad fit. When his fist hit his mouth and he sucked on it, Clay got the message.

"Why didn't you say you were hungry, buddy? I reckon milk runs out of a little half-pint belly quicker than solid food goes through my gallon-sized one." He worked quickly to get the milk and spoon out as he spoke over the cries that didn't give any sign of letting up. As soon as he had everything ready, he picked up the baby and settled back in the rocker.

This time Clay's eyes drooped lower with each rock until he stopped altogether. Forcing himself to stay awake so he didn't drop the baby or miss his mouth with the spoon, Clay thought of Cedar Bend, Kansas, and the Brady family.

"You'll like Doc and Mrs. Brady. Reckon you'll like Joanna, too. She's a mighty pretty girl. Sweet as they come. A boy called her fat once, but I set him straight pretty quick." Clay chuckled, remembering. "He went crying home to his mama with a bloody nose. Never heard him say anything bad about Joanna after that. If we'd been older, I might have come calling on her. 'Course, a girl with a fine family like that wouldn't want to pal around with the likes of me. Reckon I'd better stop walking down memory lane, don't you think, buddy?"

The baby looked up at Clay with a serious expression. If Clay didn't know better, he'd think the kid understood everything he told him. When that wheezing sound started this time, Clay was prepared. He felt like an old hand when the baby belched just like before. This time he lowered the little guy and stuck the spoon back in his mouth before a single cry sounded.

By the time Clay felt his arm go numb, Buddy's eyes closed and his breathing evened out. Holding the little guy close, Clay stood and crossed to the bed. He gladly laid his burden on the far side and crawled in beside him. He yawned as he tucked the covers around the baby. First light would come too soon for his liking, but he needed to get to the Bradys' as soon as he could. He didn't know beans about taking care of a baby, and he'd be glad enough to be rid of him.

Clay jerked awake when something hit his side. He grabbed for his six-shooter and realized he'd left it in the holster hanging on the back of a chair eight feet away. He must have been awfully tired when he went to bed to do that.

Sunshine streamed through the dirty window beside him,

lighting the cabin. A quick glance around the unkempt room brought Clay to full awareness, as did another kick in his side. The baby had turned crossways on the bed and was using him for a target.

"Hey, buddy, what're you kicking me for?" Clay put a hand on either side of the little guy and looked down at him. "Think it's past time to get up, do ya?"

Both little arms flailed in the air and a baby smile brightened the little one's face while gurgles and coos sounded like real words.

"Well now, I didn't know you could talk." Clay found himself smiling down at the baby. He touched a finger to the smooth skin just under the tiny chin.

The baby gurgled again, and Clay figured he knew what his little friend was trying to say. "I know, buddy. I overslept. 'Course I reckon that might be because I had to get up in the middle of the night and feed someone. We won't even mention that diaper. We'd better get on the road, though. We don't want Mrs. Brady to get away before we get there, do we?"

By the time Clay had the baby fed and changed, he'd given up on arriving at the Bradys' before breakfast. In fact, the sun had traveled well into midmorning by the time he saw the first sign of Cedar Bend. On the trip in, he'd given his errand a bit of thought and decided he might not be as welcome as he had been all those years ago. After all, he was a grown man now rather than a motherless boy. So he circled the town and came in across the open range to the back of the Brady house.

Clay spotted the barn first and headed toward it. He spoke to the baby. "Reckon we'd better lay low until we can see what's going on around here. What do you think about that idea, buddy?"

Sliding from his horse and slip-tying him to a tree near the back corner, Clay took the baby out of his sling and carried him into the barn. As his eyes adjusted to the muted light, Clay took inventory of his surroundings. Tack and tools hung from the weathered walls with a wide empty space where he assumed the buggy usually rested.

Doc Brady must be out making calls on his patients. Maybe that was for the best. He liked the doctor, but it was Mrs. Brady he remembered with fondness. Still, his heart pounded against his chest at the thought of seeing the woman who had been the closest to a mother he had ever known.

"Reckon I'd better not stop in and say howdy to your new ma, buddy." Clay looked into the baby's blue gaze. "For sure I'd be a big disappointment to her. You'll understand one of these days when you do something wrong and wish you hadn't 'cause you don't want to hurt your ma."

Clay dipped the last of the milk out and fed the baby. An idea took root in his mind when he saw an empty crate leaning against the far wall. As soon as the baby had given his customary belch, Clay wrapped him in a quilt and made a bed for him in the crate with all of his belongings, including the Bible. While the baby went to sleep, Clay tore the paper label from the crate and went in search of something to write with. When he'd about given up on finding what he needed, he saw the doctor's toolbox. Rummaging through it, he found the stub of a pencil.

Holding the paper against the door frame, he thought about what he wanted to say. Finally, he printed a note and replaced the pencil. "Good thing you're a sound sleeper." He spoke in a soft voice as he unpinned the baby's diaper and pinned it back with the note attached.

Carrying the crate with the baby nestled inside, Clay slipped from the barn and approached the side of the house facing the drive. Hoping Mrs. Brady didn't appear before he could get away, Clay set the crate down on the porch, gave three quick knocks on the door, and dashed across the yard to hide in the barn. He had a good view of the house and road from where he stood near the open door facing the house. Shouldn't take long for Mrs. Brady to answer her door, but Clay intended to make sure his little buddy was taken care of before he went on to Texas.

five

Clay stared at the closed door, willing it to open. Maybe no one was home. Could be Mrs. Brady and Joanna had gone with the doctor someplace. Maybe Joanna didn't live here anymore.

That last thought didn't sit well with Clay. For a reason he didn't understand, he wanted Joanna to be just the way he remembered her. Well, not exactly the same. A little older wouldn't hurt.

He shook his head and muttered, "Better toss that notion out real quick. Won't do any good to get sentimental about something that'll never be."

He concentrated on the door that remained stubbornly closed. Surely the Bradys hadn't moved. He saw the sign announcing the doc's services in the front yard facing the street. He'd clipped grass from around the posts enough times to know where to look for it.

A wagon rumbled down the dirt road, splashing water from a mud puddle before turning the corner and rolling toward town. Clay looked back at the crate on the porch. A tiny hand reached above the wooden side, and the baby's soft mews sounded. Clay knew what that meant from experience. Wouldn't be long before some real squalling started. Maybe he'd better do something.

Clay started to move out of the barn just as a buggy rolled

into the lane leading to the house. He jumped out of sight.

A tall man stepped down first. He wore cowboy boots and a wide-brimmed Stetson. Didn't look like he'd done any cowboy work in that fancy leather vest and creased denim pants, though. He lifted a little girl from the seat and then helped a lady climb down. Clay tried to remember the couple and couldn't. Every muscle in his body tensed when the family headed toward the porch and the crate.

The baby's cries intensified at that moment. The little girl ran ahead and bent over the crate. Her childish voice carried to him.

"Mama, Papa, look what I founded." She clapped her hands and turned to face her parents. "Can I keep it? Please, Papa, can I?"

"Oh, Sherm, it's a baby." The woman joined the little girl. "What do you suppose. . ." Her voice drifted off as she picked up the crying infant.

Clay watched as she cradled the little guy in the crook of her arm and gently swayed with him in a rocking motion. His cries stopped, and Clay knew his little buddy would be inspecting these new people with that intense look in his blue eyes.

The man knocked on the door, his voice a low rumble that Clay couldn't distinguish. Maybe Mrs. Brady would come now at his knock. Clay watched, holding his breath. Then he heard the woman again as she held up the paper he'd torn from the crate. "There's a note. It says his ma and pa are dead. Someone left him for Mrs. Brady. Oh, that's so sad. Who would have done this?"

The man and woman lowered their voices then. Probably

so the little girl wouldn't listen, but Clay couldn't hear either. He was ready to reveal himself at any time in defense of the little guy, but the way the woman cuddled and soothed the baby, that didn't seem necessary. They found the Bible and looked through it, then finally gathered up the baby's things and headed back to the buggy. Clay watched the woman climb in with the baby held close, as if she were laying claim to his little buddy, and he felt a sudden, unexplainable sense of loss.

As soon as the buggy turned back onto the road, Clay raced for Lucky and leaped into the saddle to follow them. No way would he let his buddy get away until he knew he'd be all right.

&

Joanna placed the freshly bathed and warmly wrapped infant in his mother's waiting arms. While her father cleaned his instruments and stored them in his bag, Joanna opened the bedroom door to call to the new father.

"Mr. Dugan, you may come in now and see your wife and child." She stepped back as the young father barreled past her.

He turned midway to the bed. "Is Margaret all right?"

Joanna giggled as the young mother spoke from the bed before she could answer. "I'm fine, Jerry. Just tired. You would be, too, if you'd done what I just did. Harder than puttin' in a day's washing, I'll tell you now."

Smothering another giggle, Joanna crossed the room to her father's side. "Dad, I think I'll walk back to town if you don't mind."

Dr. Brady snapped his black bag closed and looked at his daughter with raised eyebrows. "You sure? You've been on your feet since before daylight."

"Standing around mostly, just waiting. It's only a couple of miles. A brisk walk should do me good."

A smile crossed her father's pleasant face. "You've made some good changes, Joanna. I'm proud of you. Your mother would have been, too."

Joanna swallowed the lump that formed at the mention of her mother and smiled. "Thanks. Now, if you don't need me anymore, I'll go on."

With her father's permission granted, Joanna congratulated the Dugans and left. There'd been more rain the night before, but sunshine now streaked across the land, brightening the world in a riot of spring colors. Drops of water glistened on the new leaves of the trees and undergrowth along both sides of the road. A fresh, clean scent permeated the country air, and Joanna breathed deeply as she walked along, being careful to stay off the softer parts of the road.

She walked down Main Street, waving and speaking to one person or another as they met. She passed the future library and thought about going inside but decided she wanted to go home and change her clothing first. A couple of blocks farther brought her to the feed store. She saw a wagon parked in front but didn't see anyone outside until Mark stepped from behind the vehicle.

"Joanna, I didn't know you were coming by today."

He made it sound as if she had come to see him. "I'm on my way home. I just helped Dad deliver a baby."

"A baby." Mark smiled. "Maybe someday we'll have our own babies."

Joanna instinctively stepped back. "I don't know, Mark. I

don't think unmarried people should have children."

Mark laughed. "That's what I like about you, Joanna. You've got a real sense of humor. I meant after we're married. Isn't it about time we set the date?"

Joanna sighed. How could she come right out and tell Mark she didn't want to marry him? How could she hurt him that way when marriage to him, more than likely, was exactly what the future held for her?

A buggy rolled down the street, and she turned to watch it as an excuse to ignore Mark's unwelcome question. She recognized the buggy at the same time she saw Mariah Butler sitting on the front seat. Mr. Butler drove quickly down the street, and neither he nor his wife looked to the side. They drove away before she had a chance to call out a greeting. How strange. She hadn't realized they were home, but they must have come in the day before. She thought she saw Hope sitting between them.

Disappointed she had missed seeing her friend, Joanna scarcely listened to Mark as his voice droned on. She turned from watching the Butlers' buggy and caught sight of a lone rider going the same direction.

"Joanna, are you listening to me?" Mark asked.

"Yes, Mark, of course I am." As the horse and rider drew alongside the wagon Mark had been unloading, Joanna's breath caught in her throat. The man's white cowboy hat sat low on his forehead, with coal black hair curling beneath. His forearms and hands, strong-looking and tanned, contrasted with his light blue rolled shirtsleeves. A flood of memories filled Joanna's mind. Memories of a teen boy sitting in the back of the classroom. His smile seeming so personal when his pale blue gaze rested on her face. The same boy working for her father, cutting grass, chopping wood, running errands for her mother. Joanna's heart fluttered before reason returned.

It couldn't be Clay Shepherd. He wouldn't be riding down the streets of Cedar Bend. He probably wasn't even in Kansas. She would know, wouldn't she? As often as he filled her dreams, she would know if he were anywhere near. Surely she would.

❧

Clay caught up with the buggy just before it reached the business part of town. He held Lucky back. No need to let the man know he was being followed. They rode past the church Clay remembered attending a few times just to please Mrs. Brady. That was before he'd gotten interested in the things he heard and continued attending for his own benefit. The minister had preached about promises from a loving heavenly Father that Clay wished were true, such as granting the desires of his heart and adopting him into the family of God. The preacher claimed God was always with His children in good times as well as bad. Clay figured God wouldn't take a cowboy into His family who'd stumbled over the right and wrong line so many times he couldn't stand straight anymore. He'd never walk on those streets of gold.

Clay hadn't thought of the things he'd learned in Cedar Bend, or of the people who lived there, for a long time. Oh, sometimes he'd dream of a cute little girl who grew right along with him in his mind. But he figured she wouldn't remember him if she saw him. When his pa moved him from one ranch to another so often he couldn't keep friends, he'd learned to not even try. Only when they'd stayed in Cedar Bend a whole year had he let his guard down. And look what that had gotten him—a glimpse into heaven and a glimpse at a true family. Two things he would never experience for himself.

When Clay worked for Dr. Brady, he saw firsthand what home and family meant. Although he never let them know, he watched Joanna and her parents in their daily lives. What he saw made him envy Joanna and yet fall in love with her at the same time. He envied her because she had both a mother and father who loved and cared for her. He fell in love with her because of her gentleness, caring, and obedience to her parents.

Then Pa said it was time to move on, and Clay left Cedar Bend without ever letting Joanna know how he felt about her. He knew he would never stand a chance with a lady of Joanna's caliber. He remembered watching and listening to her sing at church. He'd never heard another voice so pretty as hers. He'd never seen anyone else who enjoyed singing as much as Joanna either. A smile always hovered around her lips when she sang, and he was certain the angels in heaven must have looked down in approval. He thought surely that's exactly the way she felt, because when she sang, Clay felt a presence of love and peace that must be God descending to take Joanna's offering.

Clay sharpened his attention on the buggy ahead when it turned onto a country road. They must be getting close to their destination. But they traveled several miles more before turning again. As Clay reached the second turn, he had a good idea where he was. When he saw the wooden arch that spanned the road, he knew. Burned on the cross board above his head were the words Circle C Ranch. Clay rode in as if he'd been planning a visit all along.

He knew three men owned the Circle C and that this was one of the largest spreads in western Kansas. One of them had a daughter that had been in his class at school. He remembered she had auburn hair and kept away from him as if he might contaminate her, but he couldn't remember her name.

That didn't matter to him. He made a quick decision as he guided Lucky toward the buggy that had stopped near the ranch house. He needed a job and a place to stay. One ranch was as good as any other to him, but this one had his little buddy, so he couldn't move on just yet. He'd talk to the boss. See if the Circle C needed a good wrangler. Just until he was sure the baby would be taken care of. Then he could go on to Texas.

six

Joanna waited until midmorning Wednesday before her father's buggy was available for her to take out to the Circle C.

"Don't stay long, Joanna," her father cautioned. "You never know when an emergency may come up."

"I won't."

Joanna pulled the door open and stepped onto the front porch just as a buggy pulled to a stop in the drive. She laughed and waved then stuck her head back inside. "I'm not going, Dad. Mariah's here."

Joanna turned back to watch Mr. Butler help Mariah from the buggy. She seemed to have something clutched in her arms as she stepped carefully down. No sooner had he turned Mariah loose than Hope leaped into her father's arms. Joanna could hear Mariah scolding the little girl. She giggled when Mr. Butler assured his wife he was capable of catching a four-year-old. Then he pulled Hope back and looked into her eyes with a stern expression. His voice drifted across the yard to Joanna.

"However, young lady, that does not give you license to jump at me before I'm ready. You must always be certain I know what you have in mind or you may find yourself in a heap on the ground with a broken arm. Is that clear?"

Hope nodded her head, dark ringlets swaying. "Yes, Papa. Now can I go see Aunt Joanna?"

He turned to his wife. "How about it, Mama? Shall I let this one go?"

Mariah's laughter sounded of happiness and contentment. "By all means."

Hope's little legs churned as soon as her feet touched the ground, and she called out, "We comed to see you, Joanna, 'cause I finded us a new brohver on your porch."

"On my porch? A new brother?" Joanna scooped the little girl up and gave her a hug. "Whatever are you talking about now?"

"We comed to talk to you. Can we keep him forever and ever?" Hope's little arms squeezed Joanna's neck. "Mama says he's yours so we haves to ask you."

Joanna turned her attention from Hope to watch Mariah and Sherman approach. Her eyes widened. Mariah indeed carried a baby wrapped in a soft blue blanket. "Mariah, what is she talking about?"

Her friend smiled as she stepped up on the porch. "May we go inside? If your father's here, I'd like to include him."

More than a little confused, Joanna nodded. "Yes, he's home." She opened the door and stepped back. "Please, go on in."

Joanna followed Mariah into the house and then called her father from his office.

While the Butlers settled on the sofa and her father took his favorite chair, Joanna set out cookies and poured coffee for the adults and a small glass of milk for Hope. When everyone had been served, Joanna sat in a wide, overstuffed chair next to the sofa. Within seconds, Hope climbed up to snuggle next to her, a cookie clutched in each hand. Joanna turned her attention to her friend and said, "All right, I'm about to burst from curiosity. Whose baby is that? Where did you get him?"

Mariah looked from Sherman to Tom Brady and back to Joanna, "We stopped by here yesterday morning about ten o'clock because I wanted to let you know we had returned home. Obviously, we missed you."

"Yes," Joanna said, "I helped Dad deliver the Dugan baby. We were gone most of the night and morning."

"Oh, how wonderful." Mariah smiled. "Are they all right?"

Joanna nodded. "Yes, they have a healthy baby boy. But so do you, and you still haven't told us where he came from."

Mariah laughed. "I assure you I'm still trying to figure that out for myself."

"I finded him." Hope squirmed in the chair. "I wants to keep him forever and ever. Can I, Aunt Joanna? Please?"

"I really don't know, Hope. Maybe if your mother tells us where she got him, we'll know more." Joanna looked at Mariah, but Sherman was the one who spoke.

"A crate was on your side porch in front of the door. Hope had already discovered the baby nestled in a bed of straw and wrapped in a quilt by the time we got to the porch. Someone left him there."

Mariah turned to Dr. Brady. "We were hoping you would take a look at him, just to make sure he's all right. Would you mind?"

"Of course not." Tom stood. "Why don't you bring him into my examining room and we'll see what we think?"

After everyone filed into the next room, Mariah handed the baby to the doctor and then watched as he laid him on the table. His examination didn't take long, but the tiny boy woke and started to cry until the doctor spoke to him in a soothing voice. The baby's expression became serious as he studied the man's face above him.

Dr. Brady wrapped him up and handed him to Mariah. "You've got yourself a fine little boy there, Mrs. Butler. He seems healthy and well cared for to me." He looked from Mariah to Sherman. "Have you tried to find the parents?"

"Oh, I forgot to tell you about the note." Mariah handed the baby to her husband who cradled him close in his arms while she dug in her handbag.

Mariah handed Joanna a folded piece of paper and watched while she opened it and read aloud, "Mrs. Brady, another boy needs your mothering. His ma and pa died in a tornado a day's ride north of here."

Joanna looked at the others, but no one spoke. Were they thinking the same thing she was? Probably not. They hadn't seen Clay Shepherd riding down Main Street yesterday. Excitement stirred in her heart at the thought of Clay outside on her porch.

Another boy needs your mothering. But even if he had written the note, where could he have gotten a baby whose parents were dead? The man she saw yesterday probably wasn't Clay anyway. Sometimes her imagination distorted her common sense, and that's more than likely what happened. Especially with Mark pressuring her to set a date for a marriage she had never agreed to in the first place.

"Joanna, is anything wrong?" Mariah's voice brought her back to the present.

"No, of course not." Joanna handed the note back to her friend. She giggled. "Here you are just back from your wedding trip and you bring a baby. You certainly have changed from that stuffy, old-maidish schoolteacher Carrie remembers, Mariah."

"That I have." Mariah laughed, and the men laughed with her. She sobered as she touched the blanket that covered the baby then smiled up at her husband. "I wouldn't go back to those days for anything, Joanna. I thought I had passed the age for a family of my own. Now look at what all God has given me."

She gave a quick laugh. "Just think, we will soon be grandparents, and here He has brought us an infant we've already come to love as if he were our own. Do you think it would be wrong for us to keep him?"

Joanna looked at her father. He shook his head. "I don't know why it would be wrong as long as there is no family."

Sherman nodded. "I've got Luke looking into that."

Tom met the gazes of his friends. "Sherman, Mariah, I can't think of any other couple who would make better parents for this little fellow. If my wife could, she would tell you to take him into your home and into your hearts and raise him as your own son. He needs a mom and a dad, and I believe your hearts are big enough to fill that role."

Joanna felt as if her father's words of approval were a sort of benediction on the Butlers becoming the baby's parents. She dabbed at moisture in the corner of her eye and giggled. "Since we are all agreed that God has given you another child, why don't you tell us what we can call him? Young Master Butler will be too much to say when he starts toddling around getting into things, don't you think?"

Mariah laughed and gave Joanna a quick hug. "My dear

friend, you do know how to lighten a mood, don't you? There was a family Bible in the crate with him. In the family pages there is an entry for Daniel S. Jacobs who was born on February 3, 1894. That makes him four months old. I think that's our baby, don't you?"

"Oh, how wonderful that you have that for him. I wish we could find out who brought little Daniel, though."

As Sherman shook hands with Dr. Brady and thanked him for his help and approval, Mariah told Joanna that since they didn't know his middle name, they were hoping to turn his middle initial into Sherman.

"Then he'll truly be yours." Joanna smiled. "And we can call him Danny until he's older."

Mariah laughed and said, "We could call him Buddy, I guess. That's what our new ranch hand called him when he asked Sherman for a job."

Joanna's heart jumped as her imagination brought to mind a young man with coal black hair and pale blue eyes astride a fine-looking black horse. She imagined him offering a gentle finger for the baby to grasp and turning that half smile she had never forgotten on the little guy before he called him Buddy. Still, as much as she wanted to, she could not bring herself to ask Mariah their new employee's name.

ⵣ

Later, Joanna busied herself getting lunch ready for her father. After they ate and he left, Joanna thought of Mariah's baby and wondered if Clay really had come back. She tried cleaning the house but gave up when she realized she had dusted her mother's occasional table three times.

"I'll go to town." She put the dust rag away, changed into

a clean dress, and straightened her hair before tying on a matching bonnet. Satisfied that she looked presentable, she started out on foot.

Sunshine flooded the land around her, and she welcomed its warmth even though she knew the hot days of summer were just ahead. When she reached Hutchinson's General Store, she crossed the street and opened the door. The bell jingled to announce her presence.

"Good afternoon." Mrs. Hutchinson looked up from some trinkets she had been arranging in a display. "How are you, Joanna?"

"Just fine."

"May I help you with anything?"

Joanna started to say she wanted to make a quilt for Mariah's new baby but stopped just in time. Mariah and Sherman would have to spread their own good news. Instead, she asked, "Do you have any batting? And I'd like to look at your fabric."

"Going to make a quilt, are you?" Mrs. Hutchinson led the way down one aisle.

Joanna smiled at how quickly one's business became public, no matter how inconsequential. "Yes, I've been thinking about making one."

Mrs. Hutchinson glanced over her shoulder as she stopped by the fabric. "Why don't you pick out the prettiest ones while I get your batting?"

"Thank you." Joanna began looking through the bolts of fabric.

"So is this for your hope chest?" Mrs. Hutchinson hadn't left as Joanna hoped. "You and Mark Hopkins haven't set the date, have you?"

Joanna shook her head. "No, nothing like that. I just found a little time on my hands this afternoon and decided to start a quilt."

Obviously discouraged by Joanna's lack of information, the woman turned away. "I see. I'll be getting that batting then."

By the time Joanna had purchased enough fabric and batting for a full-size quilt, plus several pieces of soft cotton, she had a large, bulky package to carry home.

"Sure you can handle that?" Mrs. Hutchinson asked.

Joanna grasped the bag with both arms and nodded. "Oh yes, it isn't heavy, just burdensome. I'll make it fine."

Without thinking about her route home, Joanna stayed on the same side of the street as the store and soon came to the mudhole that she'd had to wade through the other day while Mark waited on the other side. She stood looking at the muddy street. Granted, the sun had dried the standing water, but she still hated to walk through mud, no matter how shallow. Clumps of sticky clay always seemed to cling to the soles of her shoes.

A whistle sounded behind her. Joanna swung quickly to see a grinning Clay Shepherd swaggering down the street toward her. Surely a figment of her imagination.

"Miss Joanna Brady. Been a long time since I've seen you. Least ways I'm hopin' you're still a miss."

His grin widened, and her heart stopped pumping blood to her brain so that she lost all rational thought. Before she realized this was the real Clay Shepherd and not one of her dreams, he swept her up in his arms, bulky package and all. She let out a shriek that should have brought the entire town running as her arm found the only hold available—a tight clutch around Clay's neck. Before she could gather her wits, Clay strode across the mud and deposited her on the other side on dry ground.

A bit late, she found her voice. "You can't carry me. I'm too heavy."

Clay took her package from her, then stepped back and let his gaze drop to her shoes and back to her face while that half grin she had always loved lifted the corner of his mouth. He shook his head. "If that's so, I sure didn't notice. Seems to me, Joanna Brady, you've grown up into a mighty fine-lookin' woman."

seven

Joanna saw the appreciative glint in Clay's eyes, and warmth flooded her cheeks.

"Hey, Joanna, you all right?" A man who had probably seen the entire incident called from across the street.

"I'm fine." She waved and realized he wasn't the only one who had been watching. A couple stood just outside the general store staring at her. Another man rode by on a horse, his neck craned to look back. If these people were any indication, the entire town had indeed been ready to come to her aid.

She grabbed for her bag, which Clay skillfully kept from her reach. "Give me that. Everyone is staring at us."

Clay stepped around her to take his place between her and the street. His wide grin said he didn't mind the attention, but he enjoyed her discomfort. He extended his elbow for her to take and gave a short bow. "In that case, my lady, don't you think we'd better be on our way?"

"What do you think you are doing, Clay Shepherd?"

"Aha, then you do remember me." He shook his head. "For a second there, I thought you might not."

If he mentions that kiss, I know I'll die of embarrassment. Lord, is Clay the answer to my prayer? There certainly is nothing boring about him. My heart is pounding as if I've just run a mile. And he thought I had forgotten him. Little does he know how often he's visited my thoughts in the last six years, but even more so in the last two days.

Lifting her head high, Joanna started down the street toward home. How else could she get away from the stares still directed toward them? "Of course I haven't forgotten you, Clay. You worked for my father, after all."

"That's right, I did." He fell into step with her as he swung her package onto his shoulder and held it there with one hand. "How is the doctor?"

"He's fine." Joanna wondered if her heart pounded from Clay's proximity or from embarrassment over the scene he had caused in the middle of town.

"Reckon he's keeping busy doctorin' everyone?"

"Yes, he is."

Clay chuckled. "You're real talkative today, ain't ya?"

When Joanna didn't respond, he said, "Since you didn't ask, I got a job here and plan to stay for a while. You'll be seeing me around, I promise."

The breath caught in Joanna's throat. What kind of promise was that? Did he mean anything by it? She turned to see a teasing light in his clear blue eyes. Time hadn't lessened Clay's appeal. In fact, he had matured into a heart-stopping and very appealing man.

"The Circle C needed a wrangler, so here I am."

"You are the Butlers' new help? Mariah said they hired someone."

"You friends of theirs?" Clay asked.

Joanna tried to read his expression, which seemed curious, as he waited for her answer. She nodded. "Yes, Mar— Mrs. Butler is a very dear friend of mine."

"Mrs. Butler," he repeated. "I heard they just got married."

"That's true. They were married two weeks ago."

He looked forward as if in thought before he spoke in a musing voice. "I reckon that means her first husband died leavin' her with two little kids to raise."

Joanna giggled.

Clay looked at her with a wide grin. "What? I must have said something funny."

"It's just that Mariah's never been married before."

"Ya don't say?" Clay's eyebrows lifted. "Then those two little ones must belong to Mr. Butler."

Joanna giggled again. She couldn't help feeling especially lighthearted with Clay striding alongside her, carrying her package on his shoulder. If she didn't know better, she would think all her dreams had just come true. But Clay Shepherd wouldn't stick around. She imagined he was like his father, drifting from one place to another, never content to settle down like regular folks. He didn't know anything else. She couldn't expect any more from him. And wouldn't. But why not enjoy this little respite from her too-quiet life?

Looking up into Clay's handsome face, Joanna resisted the nervous urge to giggle yet again. Instead, her smile matched his as she said, "I know it sounds a little strange, but Mariah seems to attract children. I mean, she was a schoolteacher for a long time, and then she moved here to teach, and the next thing we knew, Mrs. Wainwright. . .I don't know if you remember the Wainwrights, but they were raising her niece. When they moved away, she decided she didn't want her anymore. Hope, I mean. The niece. Mrs. Wainwright always resented her sister, Hope's mother. She took Hope in when her sister died, but she never treated her right."

She shut up as soon as she saw Clay's amused expression. Why did she have to giggle and then rattle on like a magpie just because he looked so appealingly handsome?

"So Mrs. Wainwright gave Hope to Mrs. Butler?" Clay encouraged her to continue.

"No, to Mariah." Joanna flushed when he lifted his eyebrows. "I mean she wasn't Mrs. Butler then. She was still teaching school. And now she has a new baby boy that someone left on our doorstep. Probably because my dad's a doctor. But the Butlers found him, and now they want to raise him as their son. We think that's wonderful, don't you?"

"Yeah, sure."

&

Clay watched the color come and go in Joanna's smooth cheeks. Her eyes, large and dark, showed her feelings as much as the soft giggle that sounded like music to him. He had never forgotten her, but his memories were nothing compared to the real woman beside him. She was small and feminine, yet he sensed strength in her that he didn't remember. She'd grown up mighty pretty, too. Prettier than he'd expected.

They turned onto the road that led to the Bradys', and Clay wished they could walk without end, but that wouldn't happen. He needed to get back to the ranch. He had just come into town to pick up some personal things he needed. Besides, he'd see Joanna again. He'd make sure of that.

When no mention had been made of Joanna's mother before her house came into sight, Clay wanted to ask about her. But he couldn't, in case he didn't want to hear the answer.

It didn't seem right that Mrs. Brady hadn't kept the baby. The woman he remembered wouldn't have handed over a stray dog to anyone else, let alone an orphaned baby. Something was wrong, but he didn't want to hear what it was.

Clay's feet slowed and so did Joanna's as he told her a little about his work on various ranches from Texas to Nebraska. He didn't tell her about his recent experience with bank robbing, but kept his stories to the ordinary workday. Still, her eyes sparkled with interest, and he decided she was the prettiest girl he'd ever seen.

Before he wanted to, they crossed the street and stepped into the short drive leading to the Brady house. He stopped and turned to face her. "Joanna, do you reckon I could—"

"Joanna!" A man's voice yelled. Pounding footsteps sounded from the direction they had just come.

Clay heard Joanna's intake of breath as she turned to see who had called her name. He thought he heard her mutter, "No, not Mark now."

He looked, too, and saw a husky young man running toward them at full speed. Joanna's muttered words didn't make sense until he recognized an older and bigger Mark Hopkins. Years ago they'd had a few run-ins. Mark had even tried to bash his fist against Clay's face a time or two. Although Clay never stepped back from a fight he couldn't avoid, he preferred to use his quick mind and feet to get out of those he could. Especially when the odds were stacked against him like they always had been with the heavier, more muscular Mark. The same man who at the moment reminded Clay of a bull pawing the ground with both nostrils flaring. And that bull was running straight at him.

Mark crossed the road in record time, and Clay imagined he could see smoke rising from each footprint he left. "Joanna, are you all right?"

Mark stopped just short of them and pulled Joanna toward him while glaring at Clay. "Jack said he heard you scream and then go off with some man he didn't recognize. If you've hurt her, I'll—"

Clay grinned, shifted Joanna's package to his left shoulder, and offered his right hand to Mark in a gesture of friendship. "Howdy, Mark. Been a long time, hasn't it?"

Mark stared at him without touching his hand. Clay figured he hadn't recognized him yet. He felt a bit of satisfaction when he saw Joanna squirm away from Mark and step closer to him.

She crossed her arms and gave a little stomp with her foot. "Mark Hopkins, you have no right chasing after me this way. Clay didn't hurt me. I was just surprised, that's all."

"Clay?" Mark's eyes narrowed. He glanced down at Clay's outstretched hand and back to his face. "Clay Shepherd, isn't it?"

"Sure enough." Clay kept his friendliest grin in place. "I'm workin' out at the Circle C now. Reckon you'll be seein' lots of me. Just givin' Miss Joanna here an escort home from town."

Mark spit to the side before turning back to glower at Clay. "Stay away from her. You hear me, Shepherd? Joanna and me are getting married."

"That so?" Clay lifted his eyebrows in a questioning look toward Joanna.

Again her foot stomped the ground. "No, it isn't so. Mark and I are friends, that's all. I've never agreed to marry anyone."

Mark's brows drew together in a heavy dark line. He looked as if the wind had just been knocked out of him.

"Joanna, you can't mean that. What about my house? Who did you think I was building a house for?"

"I'm sorry, Mark." Her voice softened. "I never wanted to hurt you, but you just assumed I felt the same about you that you did me. I love you as a friend, Mark, not as a future husband."

Tears sprang to her eyes, and she grabbed her package from Clay before turning away. She ran to the house without looking back, but her voice drifted toward them. "I'm so sorry."

Clay didn't feel the sense of victory he had when she first told Mark off. He felt deflated somehow, like Mark looked. "Hey, man, I'm sorry. I didn't know—"

Mark's head jerked up at Clay's apology, and his eyes blazed with anger. "Just get out of here, why don't you? Face it, Shepherd, you don't belong anywhere near Cedar Bend. You never did. All you ever did was stir up trouble. Joanna's my girl, and I am going to marry her. If you come near her again, I'll rearrange your pretty-boy face for you. I promise you that."

eight

Joanna slammed the door and stood in the middle of the parlor while hot tears ran down her cheeks. She threw her bundle of quilting material at the sofa where it sat for a moment before slowly falling to the floor. She swung to the window and looked out.

Clay and Mark still stood where she left them. Mark was talking, or yelling. She couldn't understand his words, but she could hear his voice. Then he turned and stomped back toward town. Clay watched him for a moment before looking at the house.

Joanna ducked out of sight, her heart pounding. Surely he wouldn't try to talk to her, not now. She ran straight to the mirror in her bedroom. She looked a sight. Pouring a little water into the washbasin, she wet a washcloth and washed her face.

When no knock sounded at the door, Joanna laid the cloth down and crept with silent feet across the parlor to stand beside the window. She pushed the curtain aside and looked at an empty yard. Her heart sank. Clay had gone without speaking to her.

She crossed the room to sit in the wide, overstuffed chair by the sofa. As she leaned her head back and closed her eyes, she reached out to the One who had promised to be with her always. *Lord, I'm beginning to think Carrie is right. She told me*

I shouldn't wish for an exciting adventure because I might get more than I want. I can't believe Clay came today, just like in my dreams. Lord, is it wrong to want someone like Clay?

Joanna searched her heart for the answer, but none came. She wondered why Clay had shown up just when she'd been praying for excitement. Surely God would not send him to her if He didn't want them to be friends. Or maybe even more.

She thought of the way he had carried her across the mud as if she weighed no more than a child. She couldn't stop the giggle the memory brought. Clay Shepherd had certainly swept her off her feet, and he'd given her more excitement in one afternoon than she remembered having in her entire life. If she must one day marry Mark, what would it hurt to have a little fun first? She certainly would have very little afterward.

At the thought of Mark, Joanna grew sober. She had hurt Mark, and she hadn't wanted to. She did love him, but only as a friend. Why couldn't he understand that? Why did he assume she would jump at the chance to be his wife?

She bowed her head and prayed. *Lord, please forgive me for hurting Mark. If possible, could You send someone else for Mark to love? Someone who will appreciate his goodness and loyalty. He's a dear friend, and I love him in that way, but I just can't marry him. Not even someday in the future like I've always thought. I'd rather be an old maid. So please send a good wife for Mark. And Lord. . .*

Joanna stopped. How could she pray that Clay would be the one for her when she didn't know if she even wanted him? But she'd loved Clay from the first day she'd seen him when they were just children, hadn't she? Still, he was so wild. He carried an air of mystery and romance about him that called to her desire for adventure even while warning her away. She certainly would never know what to expect with Clay the way she did with Mark. Maybe that wasn't good. When they were in school, Carrie hadn't thought so, but now Carrie had found her knight in shining armor. Lucas Nolan had been just as wild and unpredictable as Clay a few years back. He'd led Carrie on a merry chase before he'd found what he was looking for.

"Come unto me, all ye that labour and are heavy laden, and I will give you rest."

The words from Matthew 11:28 spoke to Joanna's heart, convincing her. Lucas had settled down and become a regular family man after he filled the emptiness in his heart with God's love. She should be praying for Clay's salvation rather than praying for his attention.

Joanna stood and grabbed her bundle of fabric. She needed to get started on the quilt for Mariah's baby. Tomorrow would be soon enough to apologize to Mark for telling him in front of Clay she didn't want to marry him. His pride might be hurt, but he would get over her. When he met the woman God had picked out for him, he'd thank her for turning him down. As for Clay, Joanna didn't know what to do, except begin praying for him.

❧

Clay stopped at the general store and picked up the things he'd come into town to get. Then he walked to the livery where he'd left Lucky. But his mind wasn't on Lucky so much as it was on Joanna. He couldn't forget the way she'd said she was sorry and then run into the house. At first he thought her feelings were hurt, but the sound of that door slamming made him wonder. Did he say or do something that made her mad, or had her anger been directed at Mark? Maybe she was angry at both of them or maybe just herself.

Clay shrugged. He'd learned long ago that women couldn't be figured out. Soon as you thought you understood them, they'd turn the tables on you and you had to start all over again. They kept a man guessing, that was for sure. Of course he wouldn't mind studying Miss Joanna Brady one little bit. He sure was glad to know that she had never married, although he knew her marital status shouldn't matter to him. He didn't plan to stick around long enough to renew any friendships. He just wanted to make sure his little buddy had found a good home before he went south.

He paid for Lucky's stay and headed toward the Circle C. At the ranch, Clay turned Lucky toward the corral where he unsaddled him and rubbed him down. He watched the big stallion run a short distance away before turning back to whinny.

"You'll be fine." Clay grinned at the horse that was all the family he had. At the sound of his voice, Lucky trotted back for another pat. Clay obliged, then slipped through the gate and hooked it before walking toward the bunkhouse with his saddle thrown over his shoulder.

He had already spent one night at the Circle C and found the other hands to be quiet for the most part. They seemed to be a praying bunch, and he wasn't used to that. Last night and again this morning they had all gathered in the big ranch house to eat. Fifteen men sat around the long table and bowed their heads while the foreman prayed. He'd never seen anything like it. If anyone had tried that at the Crooked S back in Nebraska, they would have been laughed off the ranch. Still, these men were friendly enough without pushing past the limits he set. He hoped Lucky found his roommates as easy to get along with.

"Mighty fine-lookin' horse you got there."

Clay turned at the sound of the foreman's voice. "Howdy, Cyrus. I didn't realize anyone was around."

"I figured you'd be back about now, and I wanted to talk to ya." Cyrus fell into step with Clay. "Go ahead and stow your saddle. We can talk out here on the porch."

Clay nodded and went through the door while Cyrus sat in one of the wide, wooden chairs on the porch. One thing Clay liked about the Circle C was the cleanliness. A porch ran the entire length of the bunkhouse with white painted chairs sitting here and there. The place looked comfortable and inviting. Might be a good place to settle down if a man wanted to stay. He let his saddle and bags fall to the bare wood floor at the head of his bed and then returned outside.

He sat in the chair next to Cyrus, rested his ankle across his opposite knee, and waited. The older man leaned back and folded his hands behind his neck before he spoke. "Thought I'd give ya the lay of the land around here." He chuckled. "Reckon ya already figured out our eatin' arrangements."

Clay nodded with a grin. "First thing I usually check out is where to fill my belly."

"Can't fault ya none for that." Cyrus narrowed his eyes as he looked at Clay. "I remember your old man."

"That so?"

"Yep, kept to hisself mostly. Never caused no trouble that I can recall. Never heard any complaints about him." He nodded as if satisfied. "Reckon you're proud ta be called his son."

"I reckon so." Actually Clay hadn't thought one way or the other. He'd accepted his pa's ways, figured moving from one ranch to another was normal. He'd done the same after his father's death. Work a job until your feet get restless and then move on. That had seemed like a good philosophy to him up until now. Someone always needed a ranch hand. Like the Circle C. He looked across the yard toward the sprawling ranch house and wondered what it would be like to stay for a change. Cedar Bend was the closest to home he'd ever known. Might be a good place to put down some roots.

"Got a few broncs ta break. You done much of that?" Cyrus asked.

Clay turned from his thoughts of growing roots and faced his foreman. "Sure, I've done my share, I reckon."

"Good." Cyrus nodded. "Tomorrow we'll let ya take a turn riding fence, makin' repairs, and lookin' for trouble. Haven't had much of the two-legged kind for more'n ten years, but ya never know on a spread this size. The four-legged ones keep us plenty busy anyhow."

"How big is the Circle C?"

"Let's just say you could ride all day before comin' to the other boundary, and if ya kept goin' around the entire property, it'd take ya another three days to get back to the startin' point."

Clay whistled through his teeth. "That's a lot of land."

Cyrus chuckled. "Yep, the finest spread in Kansas. Think you'll like it here?"

"I sure hope to."

"Fine." The older man used his hands to push himself out of his chair.

Clay stopped him. "Cyrus, can you tell me something?"

"What's on your mind?"

"Just curious." Clay didn't look at Cyrus so he wouldn't know how much his answer mattered. "I used to work for the doctor. What happened to his wife?"

Cyrus rubbed the back of his neck. "She got sick. Was an invalid for a while. She died about two years ago."

The news didn't surprise Clay, but he still fought the pain it brought. He stood, being careful to keep his feelings private. "She was a good woman."

"That she was," Cyrus agreed before he changed the subject. "Hope you stay awhile. I'll get ya started with those broncs."

Clay put aside his feelings of loss as he let the excitement he always felt before riding a wild bronco glimmer deep inside. He barely listened to Cyrus and found himself nodding before he realized what he had agreed to do.

"We leave around nine to make it on time."

"On time?" He focused on the foreman's face.

"Yep, Sunday school starts at half past nine."

"Sunday school?" Clay hadn't been to Sunday school since he'd left Cedar Bend. Had he just agreed to go with Cyrus?

The old man nodded. "And church. Most everyone here goes. 'Course we take turns stayin' and workin' on Sundays so no one has to miss too often."

Clay remembered that Joanna used to sing in church. Maybe she still did. He grinned as they reached the breaking corral and another sort of excitement caught up with him. "Sure, I'll be ready at nine come Sunday morning."

"And don't be forgettin' the annual church social Saturday night." Cyrus leaned against the corral fence. "Everybody's sure to be there. Fact is, so many come that they've taken to havin' it at the Cattleman's Association Hall. Biggest place in town."

"That so?" Clay figured that meant Joanna would go. He grinned. "I'll be plannin' on it then. Thanks for lettin' me know."

He stepped on the first rung of the fence and jumped the rest of the way over, landing on his feet. Facing a wild bronco should be easy compared to a jealous Mark Hopkins come Saturday night. Clay chuckled at the thought. Good thing for him they'd be at a church social.

nine

Joanna had no sooner cleaned the kitchen on Friday afternoon than a knock sounded at the front door. She dried her
hands on her apron as she crossed the parlor. Mariah and
Carrie stood on the porch, with Hope peeking around her
mother. Mariah held her new baby son close.

"Come in." Joanna started to step back but stopped when
Hope launched herself against her and held tight. "Why,
sweetheart, what's the matter?"

The little girl looked up as Joanna bent to lift her into her
arms. Her lower lip trembled while her large dark eyes filled
with tears. "We's come to give my brohver back."

"What?" Joanna looked up at Mariah with wide eyes. "Why
would you do such a thing?"

Mariah and Carrie looked just as shocked as Joanna felt.
Mariah spoke first. "I have no idea where she got that idea."

Joanna turned and carried a now sobbing Hope into the
parlor and sat in the overstuffed chair where she could hold
the little girl on her lap. "Hope, you don't have to give little
Daniel back. Your papa had Luke check into it. They even
went to the house where your new wrangler said he'd found
your brother. Luke said it's all right for you to keep your
brother forever."

"Huh uh." Hope shook her head. "Mama said we has to
bring him back."

Joanna looked at Mariah, who seemed to be speechless at the moment. "Do you have any idea what you might have said?"

Mariah shook her head and leaned toward her little daughter. "Hope, exactly what did I say that made you think I wanted to give Daniel back?"

Hope sat up and turned a frown on her mother. "You telled Papa we's gonna go back to see Aunt Joanna and you's gonna take my baby brohver back, too."

"Oh no, honey." Mariah reached out to touch the little girl. "I didn't mean we were going to take him back and leave him. I just meant that I wanted to come back to see Aunt Joanna even though we had been here only two days ago. I love little Daniel as much as I love you and Carrie."

Mariah smiled at the young woman beside her. "None of you were born to me as most mothers have children, yet you each have been born in my heart in your own special way. I will never, as long as I live, stop thanking God for giving me such wonderful children."

She turned back to Hope. "I love you, Hope. You are my own special little girl. Carrie is my special young lady and good friend who will soon make me a grandmother." Mariah shared a smile with Carrie and then said, "And Daniel is our very special baby boy whom I already love much too much to give back."

Hope's tears stopped, and she scooted from Joanna's lap to lean against her mother's knee. She patted the baby's tiny arm. "Is we gonna keep Daniel?"

At her voice and touch, the baby opened his eyes and focused on her face. His mouth spread into a sweet baby smile as he cooed to his big sister.

Hope brightened. "Him loves me."

Mariah laughed with Joanna and Carrie. "Yes, he does." She sighed. "Oh my, I had no idea how difficult motherhood could be."

Joanna giggled. "You are doing a wonderful job, Mariah. Remember, I told you once that it was instinctive."

Carrie rested her hand on her stomach. "You make it sound so easy, Joanna. I have my doubts, though. I'm so glad Mariah is going through this now so I'll have someone to ask questions to later."

Mariah shook her head. "I fear, Carrie, that we shall have to learn together."

The three women laughed while Hope and Daniel talked and cooed to each other. Joanna watched her friends and longed for the day when she would share their so-called problems. She couldn't help wondering if her babies would have brown eyes like hers or pale blue eyes like—

"What do you think, Joanna?" Joanna's mental image of Clay cuddling their baby burst into a thousand pieces at the sound of Mariah's voice.

"I'm sorry. What did you say?"

Mariah laughed. "We were discussing plans for the library. The last time we talked, you had mentioned wanting to raise money at the town's Fourth of July celebration. Carrie just suggested we incorporate a rodeo put on by the Circle C. We'd charge an admission price and award a purse to the first three winners."

Joanna nodded. "Yes, that sounds like a very good idea. All the ranches nearby could take part. We could charge admission for the spectators, too, couldn't we?"

Mariah and Carrie exchanged amused looks. Carrie said, "That's the idea, Joanna. If we put up posters ahead of time, we should draw a good crowd."

"Back in Ohio, box suppers were quite common," Mariah said. "Do you think we could have one here?"

"Yes, we've had them before." Carrie nodded. "We'd need an auctioneer, maybe Mr. Braun."

Joanna noticed Hope had grown restless. She handed her a couple of picture books she'd had since she was a child. When the little girl settled on the floor to look at the books, Joanna leaned back and listened to her friends. The ideas they discussed could bring in a sizable income for the library if they were carried out in the right way. She had dreamed of this for so long. Now with Mariah's generosity and help, her dreams could very well become reality.

When Mariah paused for breath, Joanna said, "I want you two to know how much I appreciate all you are doing to build a library for Cedar Bend. This has been my dream, but I believe you, too, have caught the vision of what can be. However, I'd like for our library to belong to the entire town, and for that to happen, I think we need more people involved."

"Maybe we could form a sort of club with open membership to anyone interested." Mariah's eyes sparkled with enthusiasm.

"That's a great idea," Carrie said. "The more people involved the better."

Excitement grew in Joanna as she thought of the women in the community who would join. Although the library had been her idea and part of her hated to give up control, she realized she couldn't handle such a big project alone. Hard as it might be, she would have to step down and become just one of many working for the betterment of Cedar Bend.

"However," Carrie continued. "I think we need to make it clear from the start that Joanna is in charge."

"Yes, of course," Mariah agreed. "I took for granted that she would be."

Joanna met the smiling faces of her friends, and her heart filled with love for them both. What did anyone ever do without friends? How could Clay drift from place to place without forming attachments? She shook off the invasive thoughts of Clay Shepherd that continually plagued her and concentrated on Mariah's voice.

"We could have a quick meeting at Saturday evening's social when everyone is together. Our first order will be to make Joanna our official librarian." She lifted a questioning gaze to Joanna. "That is unless you have any objections."

"No, no, I don't suppose I do." Joanna turned to her friend. "Do you think I can handle the job? I've only been to one actual library a long time ago."

Mariah laughed. "I think you'll do fine."

"Great." Carrie stood. "Since that's decided, Hope and I have business elsewhere."

Hope jumped up from the picture books and ran to Carrie, taking her hand. "We's gonna go on a secret."

"Yes, we are." Carrie placed a finger across Hope's lips. "Let's not tell or it won't be a secret."

"Awright." Hope nodded and pulled Carrie toward the door. "Bye, Aunt Joanna. Bye, Mama. Bye, baby brohver."

Joanna and Mariah both told her good-bye and watched as

Carrie closed the door behind them. Mariah stood with the baby. "I believe my son has gone to sleep. Would you mind if I lay him down?"

Joanna jumped up. "No, of course not. You may put him on my bed. Does he roll over yet?"

"Not yet. But let's put a pillow on each side just in case."

After they settled the sleeping baby on the bed and tiptoed from the room, Joanna asked Mariah, "Do you know what your daughters' secret is?"

Mariah laughed. "I have a good idea. I'm sure they are on a mission to buy a gift for a certain little brother they both dote on without shame."

"Oh, how sweet." Joanna smiled. "Carrie has certainly had to make some adjustments in her life, hasn't she? Going from an only child to having not only a stepmother but two young siblings in less than a month must make quite a difference."

"I'm sure it does." Mariah sat at Joanna's table and accepted the cup of tea she offered. "She called herself a selfish little brat once, but I haven't seen any selfishness manifested lately. She loves Hope and treats her as if she's always been her little sister."

"God had great things in store when He brought you to us, didn't He, Mariah?"

"Oh yes, God and Kansas have been good to me." Mariah smiled. "But enough about me. I want to know what's troubling my dear friend."

"Me?"

"Yes, Joanna, you. I'm not blind, deaf, or dumb. I've been watching you slip off into a world of your own even as we visited this afternoon. Something is on your mind, and it isn't just the library, as important as I know that is to you."

Joanna giggled. "My, but you are perceptive. However, I really couldn't say that anything is wrong. On the contrary, so much is right. The library is off to an absolutely marvelous start, thanks to you. I've lost weight and feel better than I can ever remember. I have the dearest friend anyone could ever ask for. How could anything be wrong?"

Mariah sipped her tea and gave Joanna an assessing look. Joanna lifted her own cup and took a long, bracing sip. How could she feel so guilty when she hadn't lied? She just hadn't confessed the whole truth. But did she have to? Did she have to tell her friend of the longing in her heart for excitement? Carrie hadn't understood, and Carrie was her age. How could an older, wiser, more settled friend understand the restless feelings that sometimes seemed to overwhelm Joanna?

Finally, under Mariah's steady gaze, Joanna looked up and giggled. "You know me too well."

"It isn't hard to see you have something on your mind."

Joanna sighed. "It's nothing really. I just feel so restless sometimes. Mark Hopkins thinks I'm his girl, and he's even building me a house."

"That's wonderful. Mark is such a nice young man." Mariah's quick smile faltered as Joanna shook her head.

"But it isn't wonderful, and that's part of the problem." She sighed again. "I don't love Mark. I mean, I do, but only as a friend. I told him that. The other day when Clay walked me home from the store. I told him right in front of Clay that I don't want to marry him."

Joanna covered her face with both hands until she heard Mariah's soft laughter.

She looked up to see a teasing light in her friend's eyes. "Why, Miss Joanna Brady, I do believe you lead a more exciting life than I knew. Would this Clay you mentioned be Sherman's new wrangler?"

Heat filled Joanna's cheeks as she nodded.

A light seemed to ignite behind Mariah's expressive eyes, and she laughed aloud. "Oh, I can't believe this. Clay Shepherd. I am so dense to not put two and two together when I first heard his name. Don't I recall being told a secret story about a first kiss under the mistletoe?"

"Mariah, don't breathe a word." Joanna's eyes widened at the thought.

"Of course I won't." Mariah reached across the table and covered Joanna's hand with hers. "What you tell me in confidence will always remain between only the two of us." She smiled. "Clay Shepherd is a very handsome young man, Joanna. And you say he walked you home?"

Joanna nodded. "I'm going to tell you something, Mariah, in confidence. I've been praying."

When she paused, Mariah nodded in encouragement. "That's always a good thing, Joanna."

"Maybe. I mean, it could depend on what you pray for." Joanna pushed her teacup from one hand to the other before she finally spoke. "I've been praying for God to send me someone exciting. Someone dashing and romantic."

Joanna lifted hesitant eyes to look at her friend who sat staring at her. Finally, Mariah said, "You mean someone like Clay Shepherd?"

"Oh yes." Joanna released the words on a rush of breath she hadn't realized she'd been holding.

"Oh, my dear." Mariah again touched Joanna's hand. "Are you sure the young man is a Christian?"

Joanna's gaze dropped to her cup and to her friend's hand on hers. Now that Mariah had voiced her secret concern, she knew she would have to face it. How could Clay be a Christian when he'd led the life of a drifter, going from ranch to ranch with no place to call his own? Yet, why couldn't he be? She had prayed so hard. God could not make a mistake. He would send the very best, and He had sent Clay, hadn't He?

When Joanna didn't answer, Mariah's soft voice spoke to her heart. "My dear friend, be very careful. Don't allow the enemy to attack your Christian faith through this man. No matter how appealing he may seem, no matter how exciting, you must be certain that he is a child of God first. I will be praying for you."

ten

By Saturday afternoon Joanna had seen neither Mark nor Clay since the afternoon Clay had walked her home from town. Using a large package of dried apples, she made a couple of pies for the church social that evening. When the top crust turned golden brown, she pulled the pies from the oven and set them in the middle of the table to cool.

A glance at the clock told Joanna she needed to start getting ready. After a relaxing bath, she dressed in a new royal blue dress she had made herself. The color complemented her dark hair, making her skin appear smooth and unblemished. She brushed her hair until it shone then put it up, leaving short ringlets to hang down on either side.

When she looked in the mirror she scarcely recognized herself since she rarely took such pains with her appearance. She batted her eyelashes at her reflection. "Why, Miss Brady, you take my breath away."

"Mine, too." Her father's voice sounded behind her.

Joanna turned with an embarrassed giggle. "Don't you dare make fun of me. I was just complimenting myself since I don't even know if I have an escort."

Her father frowned. "No escort? For the loveliest girl in town? I assumed you would be going with Mark."

"Yes, so did I." Joanna shrugged as if she didn't care. Which she didn't really, except that she didn't like the idea of going alone and she didn't want Mark's feelings hurt. If she saw him tonight, she would make certain to apologize. Now she answered the question in her father's eyes. "We had a few words the other day, and I haven't seen him since."

"Oh, that's too bad, especially if you have to go with your old dad." Tom Brady turned from her open door. "I'll hurry and get changed. By the way, were those pies on the table for the social?"

"What do you mean *were*?" Joanna hurried toward the kitchen. "There had better be two uncut pies still on the table."

Her father's laughter told her before she saw the pies that he had been teasing her.

She decided to return the favor. She smiled at him. "I see you are in a good mood. Does this mean you have a date for the social tonight?"

His dark eyes danced with merriment. "From the way you've been talking, I may have to escort my own daughter."

"You mean you didn't ask Mrs. James?" Joanna tried to keep her expression innocent.

"As a matter of fact. . ." her father began then stopped.

Joanna's eyes widened. He wouldn't.

The doctor grinned as he finished his long, drawn-out pause. "I didn't."

"Oh, Dad. Can't I ever get the better of you?"

His laughter drifted to her as he turned toward his room. "Not if I can help it."

Joanna had the pies packed in a box and her father was just coming out of his bedroom when someone knocked at their front door. "I'll get it," he called to her.

When the door opened and she heard the murmur of

men's voices, Joanna went into the parlor. Mark clutched a spray of white daisies, which he held out to her with a wide smile on his face.

"Here, I thought you might like these."

Mark had brought her flowers? Joanna took the daisies and held them while she fought the urge to feel Mark's forehead for fever. "Thank you, Mark. I'll put these in water."

"I'll help you."

When Mark followed her to the kitchen, she thought about telling him she didn't need help, but then she remembered the pies. He might as well carry them. Besides, this would give her a chance to talk to him in private.

She took a glass from the cabinet and pumped water into it. While she arranged the flowers, she said, "Mark, I want to apologize for the other day. I shouldn't have spoken to you the way I did. I could have waited until we were alone to tell you how I feel."

"Don't worry about that, Joanna. I know you were just upset." Mark leaned against the counter. His smile seemed as confident as ever.

Didn't he understand? What could she say to get through to him? She started to speak when her father called to them to hurry or they'd be late for the social.

"Mark, do you mind carrying the pies?" Joanna slid the box across the table.

"Course not." He sniffed as he picked up the box. "Mmmm apple. Did you make these for me?"

"Just be glad she made them." Dr. Brady spoke from the doorway. "If I'd baked them, you wouldn't want even a taste."

Mark laughed with the doctor, and Joanna swept past

the men and out the door. At least Mark appreciated her pies. Not that it did anything to endear him to her. She had spent the last three hours making herself presentable for the evening's activities and not one word or even a noticeable look of appreciation did she get. Only her pies were worthy of that honor.

Since the Cattleman's Association Hall had been built on the edge of the business district within an easy walk of the doctor's house, they decided to leave the horse and buggy at home. Mark balanced the box containing the pies while he walked beside Joanna. Her father trailed behind.

With Mark talking about a recent increase in the cost of grain and how that affected the farmers and cattle ranchers, Joanna relaxed. She might be bored, but at least he wasn't trying to push her into marriage.

The streets were lined with wagons and buggies, and several families and couples on foot headed toward the hall. Joanna and Mark spoke to nearly everyone as they joined those going inside the large lighted building.

Joanna took the pies from Mark, thanked him for carrying them, and headed for the already groaning table of food.

"Here, let me clear some room." Mrs. James smiled at Joanna before moving several pies and cakes closer together. "This looks like one of our largest turnouts."

"There's certainly enough food." Joanna looked at all the pies, cakes, and other goodies on the table. She saw meat dishes and vegetables. There were more bowls of potato salad than she wanted to count.

"And more coming in, but your pies are always my favorite." Mrs. James patted Joanna's arm. "I hope I get a piece."

"Why, thank you, Mrs. James." Someone jostled against Joanna, and glad for the interruption, she turned to greet another woman from church. She liked Mrs. James but always felt uncomfortable with her. While she wouldn't mind if her father remarried, she wanted him to find someone he could love, and she hadn't noticed that he had special feelings for Mrs. James, although the woman obviously admired him.

As Joanna moved away from the ladies gathering around the food table, she looked across the room. Why her gaze landed on a tall, dark-haired young man with an appreciative glint in his eyes and a half smile on his face, she didn't know. Why Clay Shepherd was in attendance at the church social, she also didn't know. She certainly hadn't expected to see him. Her heart tripped in her chest, and she looked away.

"Hello, Joanna."

She started at the sound of Mariah's voice, and a flood of color filled her cheeks. Joanna hoped Mariah hadn't noticed where her attention had been.

"Hi. I didn't realize you were here. Where are your children?"

"Daniel is with Carrie, and Sherman has Hope." Mariah glanced across the room where Clay stood with a couple of men from the Circle C before her gaze met Joanna's. "I see our new wrangler is here."

"Your new wrangler?" Joanna looked up at her friend with wide, innocent eyes. "Oh, you mean Clay Shepherd."

"You knew perfectly well who I meant. And you knew he was here, too."

Joanna sighed. "Yes, I suppose I did."

"Just please be careful. You are a dear friend, and I don't want you hurt." Mariah glanced back toward the men. "Mr.

Shepherd is a very handsome young man, and he has just the right amount of cowboy charm that could easily capture a young lady's heart. I saw him break a wild bronco the other day. There was something about man and beast that seemed to fit. Maybe the same wild streak runs through both, making them resist the confining reins."

"I know you're right. I promise to be careful." Joanna felt as if her heart might break. She had been infatuated with Clay and his free spirit for so long. She had never forgotten him, and she never would. She almost wished he had not returned. He had been only a childhood memory before, while now he stood less than thirty feet away, an appealing man who seemed as aware of her as she was of him.

She chanced another peek at Clay and wished she hadn't when his smile widened and he winked. Joanna's heart pounded so hard against her rib cage that she had to take a deep, calming breath. If she could just keep from looking at Clay, she'd be all right.

"Joanna, I wanted to tell you"—Mariah slipped an arm around Joanna's shoulders and turned her away from Clay— "Carrie and I have already spoken to several of the ladies, and they seem quite interested in our plans for the library."

"That's wonderful." Joanna tried to concentrate on Mariah's voice as she suggested that Joanna set up a planning meeting while the ladies were interested.

She promised she would. Just then, Pastor Carson's booming voice welcomed everyone. After he prayed, he said, "We'll start off tonight with some games. If you don't want to join in, please remain outside the circle so no one gets hurt. For those who would like to play, let's gather in the middle of the room and start a brisk game of 'Captain Jinks.'"

Mark appeared beside Joanna at that moment, ready to whisk her off to play in the musical games.

Pastor Carson's voice rang out. "Grab a partner, and let's all sing together."

As soon as the circle formed, those playing and several standing to the sides of the large room joined their voices in singing, "Captain Jinks of the horse marines, we clap our hands beyond our means."

At that point everyone brought their hands together in one loud clap. The next stanza had the men swinging their partner.

"And swing that lady while in her teens, for that's the stout of the army."

Next they all joined hands and skipped to the left in a circle as they continued to sing. Then the words "Captain Jinks, the ladies' knight, the gentleman changes to the right" had the men and women changing places, which gave Joanna a new partner. This man, one of the cowboys from the Circle C, swung Joanna before they promenaded around the circle.

The game continued in the same way until Joanna found herself next to Clay. He swung her around, and they began the promenade. Although she had been well aware of him, she had lost track of how quickly they would become partners. He grinned at her, and while everyone else sang, he leaned close and said, "I thought you'd never get here."

Joanna tried to ignore the flutter his words caused in her midsection and kept her gaze on the couple in front of them. She tried to remember Mariah's warnings instead of letting herself give in to the thrill of being so close to Clay. Granted, he was at their church party, but that didn't mean he was a Christian, and she needed to remember that fact.

"Will you be my partner for the next game?" Clay asked.

Joanna missed her step, and Clay tightened his hold on her.

She looked across the circle at Mariah, but her friend didn't seem to notice her predicament. She glanced into Clay's blue eyes fringed with long, black lashes and thought she had never seen any man so handsome. Why would he waste his time on her? She gave up trying to sing and nodded. He grinned.

When the promenade stopped and they all clapped their hands, Clay leaned close and said, "You sure are pretty to-night, Miss Brady."

With the loud clap ringing in her ears, Joanna thought she might have misunderstood his words, but she recognized the admiration in his eyes. He slipped his arm around her waist to swing her, and she forgot to say thank you as she had intended. Instead, she stared up at him, holding his left hand with her right and clutching his shoulder with her left.

She followed the motions as they skipped. The words came from memory, so she sang with the others, but she and Clay might as well have been alone, for that's the way she felt. Then Clay switched to her right side and she had another partner.

When the original partners were back together, Pastor Carson called a pause.

❧

Clay stayed back, letting Mark monopolize Joanna during the break. He'd watch, see how things were between the two of them. After all, if Joanna really cared for Mark, he wouldn't step between them. But the second time Joanna looked his way while Mark talked to her, Clay decided he had waited long enough.

He saw Pastor Carson stand and figured he was about to call for another game, so he crossed the room and stopped by Joanna. "Looks like the next game is starting."

Joanna took a step back and told Mark she had promised to be partners with Clay for the next game. Before Mark had a chance to react, Joanna took Clay's arm and pulled him away.

Clay figured Mark would have liked nothing better than to bloody his nose at that moment, so he flashed his friendliest smile at the angry guy and followed Joanna. They played "Skip to My Lou," and Clay kept a close eye on Joanna after the first skipper tried to steal her from him. To play the game right, he couldn't hold Joanna's hand, but he thought about breaking the rule when Mark ended up in the center of the circle. As expected, Mark tried to steal Joanna, but Clay blocked him so he had to move on to someone else. Clay ignored the glare Mark sent his way and grinned because Joanna didn't seem to notice.

Clay hadn't had so much fun in a long time. Associating with church people wasn't so bad. He might even enjoy going to church in the morning. After all, Joanna would be there.

When the game ended and Pastor Carson prayed a short prayer over their dinner, Clay took Joanna's elbow and steered her toward the table. "I've been eyeing that food. Reckon we can get a bite of something?"

Joanna giggled. "We'd better hurry or it might all disappear."

"You think so?" Clay smiled at her. He wouldn't mind just looking at her instead of eating. He couldn't remember ever seeing a prettier girl. Her eyes were like two drops of shiny dark chocolate with beautiful, long, dark lashes. In contrast, her skin was smooth and olive toned with a touch of color in each cheek. She had put her hair up in some fancy style, and while he couldn't find any prettier in the room, he liked it better hanging down to the middle of her back and swinging free. Of course, he knew better than to tell her that. In fact, she'd probably be shocked if she knew what he was thinking.

They got in line, and Clay helped Joanna fill her plate, although she said she couldn't eat so much. "I'll be as big as the side of a barn if I eat everything you're trying to put on my plate."

Clay laughed and dropped the mound of potato salad on his plate instead of hers. He spoke low so no one else could hear. "Reckon it don't matter how much you eat, darlin'. You're still the prettiest girl in this hall."

Color flooded Joanna's cheeks, proving to him that he was right. He could look the world over and never find a more beautiful woman. Nor a sweeter one. Yep, Miss Joanna Brady could wrap him around her little finger without half trying.

"Joanna," a middle-aged woman stepped between them. "Mariah's been telling me you intend to start a library here in town. Is that right?"

"Yes, it is."

Joanna turned to the woman, and Clay stepped back. He didn't see them coming, but as soon as Joanna moved away from the table, five or six other women surrounded her, all talking about a library. He glanced to the side, trying to find a place to get away where he could eat. Then he saw Hopkins bearing down on Joanna from across the room.

"How will you display the books?"

"Won't you need a sign put out front so everyone will know the house is a library?"

"What about renovations on the house?"

Clay heard the ladies as he watched Mark weaving his way closer. Then Clay got an idea that would be sure to win Joanna's attention. He stepped back to her side.

"Excuse me, ladies, but I couldn't help hearing your conversation." Clay turned his most charming smile on the older ladies before letting it rest on Joanna. "I've done some carpenter work before. If you are in need of shelving, I'd be glad to donate my time to such a worthy cause as a library."

At the same time that Mark reached the group, Joanna turned and smiled at Clay. "That would be wonderful. As soon as we get some lumber, you can get started."

With the approving voices of the older ladies surrounding him, Clay almost forgot Mark stood glaring at him. He looked into the smiling face of the woman he just might care for enough to put down those roots he'd been thinking about and grinned.

eleven

Joanna couldn't have been more pleased. The library would soon become a reality. Her love of reading had been the catalyst that spawned the idea to provide Cedar Bend with enough books to satisfy everyone in the area. Now many others had joined her cause. Even Clay.

"Back off, Shepherd." Joanna turned at Mark's growl. The scowl on his face looked almost frightening. "You're just trying to get in good with Joanna. If she needs anything done for her library, I'll do it."

Clay simply shrugged with an amused expression on his face. "Reckon that's up to Miss Brady."

Joanna was vaguely aware of the startled reaction coming from the women surrounding them. Several of them stepped back. Some gasped. Mariah had been standing to the side listening while Joanna talked with the ladies. Now she stepped forward.

"Mark, I'm sure there's plenty of work to share for the library."

"I don't intend to share with the likes of him." Mark scowled.

Clay grinned.

Joanna wondered if he ever took anything seriously. Had Clay breezed back into town only to have some fun at their expense? Maybe his attention had just been a big joke after all.

"You want to step outside and settle this?" Joanna heard

the threat in Mark's voice.

Clay didn't seem to. He looked down at his heaping plate of food with a wistful expression before looking back at Mark. "Well now, Hopkins, to tell the truth, I'd much rather eat my dinner."

"You scared I'll mess up your pretty face?"

"Mark Hopkins, you stop this right now." Joanna turned toward her longtime friend. "There's no need to fight. Like Mariah said, we'll have plenty of work for everyone to do."

"Sorry, Joanna, this thing's between me and Shepherd. Doesn't have anything to do with your library. This has been building for a long time."

Mark's angry gaze never left Clay's face. Joanna wondered how Clay could act so unconcerned. He kept a pleasant expression as he tried to talk his angry rival out of making a scene. "You know, maybe we oughta drop this, Hopkins. Seems to me a church social just ain't the right place to settle differences."

"He's right, Mark." Mariah tried to intervene again. "Let's calm down and forget this unpleasantness ever happened."

So far the men had kept their voices low so only those standing close enough to hear knew of the confrontation. Joanna didn't know what she would do if Mark didn't back down. Clay obviously didn't want to fight. He'd tried being friendly and he'd tried to talk Mark out of fighting. But Mark refused to give up. If she'd had any doubts before about her feelings for Mark, she didn't now. If he ever calmed down enough to see reason, she planned to tell him straight out that she didn't want him pursuing her ever again. She'd had enough.

Mark gave Clay one last hard glare and nodded toward the back door of the hall, not far from where they stood. "I'm going outside. We'll soon see if you're man enough to follow."

When Mark took off for the door, Clay let out a sigh and shook his head. He grinned at Joanna as he handed her his plate. "Can you hold this for me, Joanna? I'm powerful hungry, but I reckon I still will be when I get back."

"You aren't going out there, are you?" Joanna took the plate and balanced it with her own. "He's angry, Clay. You might get hurt."

Clay shrugged and looked from Joanna to the other ladies. "I apologize to all you nice ladies for this. But I don't reckon your friend's gonna cool down much standin' around waitin' on me. Might as well get this over with instead of putting it off." He started away, then glanced over his shoulder with another grin and said, "I don't reckon Mark ever did like me much."

Joanna watched the back door close behind Clay and click with a decisive sound. She let out a strangled cry and shoved the two full plates onto the corner of the food table before running to the door.

⁂

Mark stood in the back alley behind the hall. Clay saw him as soon as he stepped outside, even though the sun had already set. He paused on the landing before stepping down the stairs. "Hey, Hopkins, we don't have to do this, you know."

"If your yellow streak's showing, just say so," Mark taunted him.

"Well, it isn't that I'm exactly scared," Clay drawled. "I'm just thinking about Joanna and how she might feel. Have you stopped to think that these churchgoing ladies might not like having a fight break out at their evening social? Could put a damper on their fun, don't you think?"

Clay kept moving toward Mark as he talked, trying to reason with the other man. Mark had hit him once when they were kids, and Clay figured the husky man had grown even more powerful through the years. He really didn't relish getting his face bashed in, but he figured he could stand pretty much anything for Joanna. Besides, maybe if Mark worked off some anger, he might also work out whatever it was that had been bothering him since he'd first laid eyes on Clay more than six years ago.

By the time he realized his talking wouldn't do any good, he was standing just outside Mark's reach. He saw Mark coming as the heavier and slower fellow lunged with his fist doubled. Having the advantage of being quick on his feet, Clay sidestepped, and Mark walked past without touching him.

Trouble was, Mark didn't like to miss, so he grew even angrier. Clay didn't want to hit Mark unless he had to, so he kept dodging the other man's big fists. Maybe in time his anger and the force he put behind each thrust of his fist would wear him down if Clay could keep a close eye on him and stay out of his way.

Mark and Clay had danced around in a circle so that when the back door of the hall burst open Clay had a clear view of the landing. For just a moment, Joanna stood framed by the doorway with the light from the room spilling out behind her. He paused, unable to look away as she ran down the stairs.

He started to call out to her to stay back. In his anger, Mark might accidentally hurt her. But at that moment a big fist blocked his view and pain exploded in his head.

In an instant, Joanna brushed past Mark and knelt beside Clay. "Are you all right?"

Clay tried to focus on her voice. Joanna wasn't nearly as pretty with her face blurred, but her voice still sounded like music to him.

"He's fine, Joanna. Why don't you step back and let me take a look. This isn't the first time a man got a black eye." Dr. Brady knelt beside Clay. "You go on over there with Mariah and Carrie."

Clay's thinking seemed as fuzzy as his vision, but he answered the doctor's questions and let him look in his eyes. He figured Mark would claim Joanna since he'd won the fight. Of course, maybe she wouldn't let him. After all, she had run to Clay first thing. That must mean something.

"Doesn't appear to be too bad. Didn't even get knocked out, did you?" the doctor asked.

Clay started to shake his head, but the movement didn't help either his vision or the pain. He grinned. "My pa always said my head was hard."

Dr. Brady laughed and helped Clay stand with Sherman Butler's help. "I'll get a cool compress for that eye. We expect to see you in church in the morning," he told Clay.

Cyrus spoke up. "He done agreed to that."

"Good." The doctor turned to Pastor Carson, who stood watching. "I think the show's over. If you can get your congregation back inside, the party can go on."

"Well, boy, you want ta tell me what happened out here?"

Cyrus took Clay's arm and led him away from the others who were heading inside.

Clay saw Mark with Joanna, although they didn't seem very happy. When the door closed behind them, he turned to Cyrus. "Would you be satisfied if I said I walked into a fist that had a little more punch than I expected?"

"Nope."

Clay sighed. "I didn't figure you would. The fact is, Cyrus, I don't rightly know what happened. Hopkins might have a better idea. If he even knows."

"Wouldn't be over a girl, would it?" Cyrus persisted. "Maybe Doc Brady's daughter?"

Clay's grin turned into a grimace as the pain shot to his eye. "Miss Brady is mighty pretty, but like I already said, I don't know. Mark never went to school when we were kids, but I saw him at Doc Brady's some when I worked there. Maybe he wanted my job."

Cyrus nodded. "Or maybe the doc's daughter."

The door opened and Dr. Brady stepped out. Clay watched him descend the stairs, glad his vision seemed to be coming back. "I would like to apologize for my part in the ruckus. It wasn't my idea for anyone to get hit."

"Least of all yourself, huh?" The doctor laughed. He applied a cool, damp cloth to Clay's eye. "Hold this against the swelling for a while. When you get home, you might want to apply another cold compress. You going back inside?"

Clay looked toward the hall and thought of Joanna with Mark. He gave a little shake of his head. "Nah, I'll head on back to the ranch."

"Well then, I'll get back inside. My daughter is mad as a

hornet. I imagine we'll go home early."

"Mad?" Clay couldn't resist asking. "At who?"

The doctor laughed. "Right now either a couple of young men or the entire state of Kansas. I'm not sure which it is."

When Clay fetched his horse, he felt comfort in Lucky's welcoming whinny. He'd sure made a mess of the evening, although he wasn't sure what he'd done wrong. A fight with Hopkins hadn't been in his plans. He'd just wanted to see Joanna again. He'd wanted to play some games with her as his partner and get a glimpse of what it meant to live a normal life where people stayed in one place. Where they got to know each other and developed friendships that lasted a lifetime.

Maybe putting down roots wasn't for him. He remembered Mrs. Brady told him once that God had a plan for everyone. Did that include him? Did God care if he ever had a family, or was he destined to ride the range for the rest of his days, moving from ranch to ranch and from state to state just the same as his father had done?

He patted his horse on the shoulder and swung into the saddle. "I don't know what's down the road for us, Lucky, but I'm sure glad I've got you to carry me there."

twelve

Clay sat on the backseat at church the next day and watched Joanna lead the singing. She'd always had the prettiest voice he'd ever heard, and that hadn't changed. What had changed was that she had grown into a beautiful, confident woman.

She looked up and turned toward him as her voice carried clearly to the back row. He started to smile, but she quickly looked away almost as if she didn't want to see him. She probably didn't. After the ruckus he and Mark had caused the evening before, she might never want to see him again. He figured the church people were being mighty forgiving to let him inside their church. Of course, they probably thought he needed to be there even more after the mess he'd made of their party.

After Joanna sat down, Clay concentrated on what the pastor had to say. Since he didn't have a Bible, he listened while the minister read several verses from the third chapter of John. One that stuck in his mind said, "Verily, verily, I say unto thee, Except a man be born of water and of the Spirit, he cannot enter into the kingdom of God."

Pastor Carson explained that the kingdom of God meant heaven and all of eternity that would follow. He said man had been born in sin and that made him a sinner from the minute he came into the world.

Clay looked at the Butlers who sat near the front. He could see his little buddy with his head against Mariah's shoulder while she patted his back. He'd kept an eye on him every chance he got and could already see the tiny baby thought the Butlers were his ma and pa. Clay had seen their little girl give the baby a kiss more than once and knew she loved him. Mr. and Mrs. Butler did, too. He felt sure of it. Even Carrie and her husband treated him as if he'd been born into the family.

The minister's words reached him again. "And how can we be born again? In John 14:6, Jesus said, 'I am the way. . .no man cometh unto the Father, but by me.'"

Clay listened as the old message of salvation became a new idea in his mind. He'd done his share of sinning, he knew that. He'd found little forgiveness from those he'd wronged, though. So the idea that the Creator of all would freely forgive him for every wrong thing he'd ever done if he would only ask just didn't make sense. Sure would be nice.

When the preacher stopped talking, Joanna stepped forward to lead another song. Clay enjoyed singing, but he mostly watched Joanna as she sang "Just as I Am," her sweet voice rising above the congregation's.

When the song ended, the pastor prayed and people began leaving. Clay hesitated when he saw Mark head for the front and Joanna. But when Joanna stepped to the far side of the piano to speak to the pianist, Mark turned and started back down the center aisle. Clay slipped out the door into a bright early June day.

"Ridin' back out with us?" One of the ranch hands walked past with a friendly smile.

"Nah," Clay shook his head. "I'll be out later."

"All right. See ya then."

As Clay started toward Lucky, a cat ran past with a mongrel dog hot on its trail. He grinned at the sight and at the racket of the cat's yowls of alarm and the dog's barking. But his grin disappeared when the cat darted between the legs of a horse hitched to a wagon. The horse let out a frightened whinny and reared, jerking the reins from a woman who appeared to be alone. Clay broke into a run and hoped the horse didn't bolt before he got there.

The horse came down with a twist and headed straight toward Clay. Five running steps brought Clay close enough to grab the horse's neck and swing onto its back. Leaning forward, he grabbed the reins and soon had the runaway horse under control.

"Thank you, mister." The woman ran to the side of the wagon.

Clay slid from the horse. "No problem, ma'am."

He ran his hand down the horse's front leg and lifted its foot. Just as he thought. A shoe had come loose. He looked up at the middle-aged woman. "This needs to be taken care of."

"Oh dear," she glanced down the road. "Brother Landon has already gone. I hate to take him from his Sunday dinner."

Several men and women stood watching and offering advice, although none had the necessary equipment to fix the horseshoe. Clay released the horse and handed the reins to the woman.

"That's all right. I'll stop on my way and let Landon know. I'm sure he'll come right away." Clay gave the woman a reassuring grin as he turned away.

Ten minutes later, Jack Landon, Cedar Bend's blacksmith, headed back to the church while Clay turned his horse in the opposite direction. Lucky ambled down the dirt road that led through the business part of town, and Clay thought about the woman he had helped. A sense of satisfaction warred with his restless spirit. He wondered why he didn't just turn south at the next street and keep on going. Texas still waited with plenty of ranches and a bunk for sleeping. He could stop by the Circle C and pick up what little he had there. Shouldn't take long.

Then he remembered those roots he'd been wanting to put down. He thought of his little buddy and wondered how it would be to have a son of his own. One thing was for certain. If he had a son, he wouldn't want him raised the way he had been—always on the move and never able to retain a lasting friendship. He'd spent only one short year in Cedar Bend, yet he'd lived here longer than he'd lived in any other place. Long enough to make an enemy.

He chuckled as he thought of Mark's frown when he'd seen him walk into church with the other cowboys. Reckon Mark wouldn't miss him if he left. Probably no one would. Joanna's wide brown eyes entered his mind accusingly. Okay, so maybe he'd made one friend. Joanna might miss him for a while, but it wouldn't be long until she married Hopkins anyway. Just save him the trouble of seeing it happen if he left.

A woman walked ahead of him down the road. He stopped Lucky and sat watching. A slow grin spread across his face and he nudged Lucky forward until he rode beside her.

"Mornin', Miss Brady." Clay grinned down at the sweetest sight he'd ever seen. "Or is it afternoon already?"

Joanna's face registered surprise, delight, and then a slight frown within the space of only a moment before she turned away. "I believe it's straight up noon."

"That so?" Clay kept pace with her. He liked sitting above her where he could watch the sunlight brighten the red highlights in her dark hair. "Sure is a pretty day."

"That's because it's early June. You won't like the bright sun in another month when there's no rain."

Clay laughed. "Reckon not. Good thing I'm not a farmer."

Joanna turned to face him with her fists planted on her hips. "Clay Shepherd, why are you following me?"

Clay admired the flash of anger in her dark eyes. A strong emotion he refused to name filled his heart. All he knew was that he wanted his future sons to have dark brown eyes just like the ones currently glaring at him, which were the prettiest he'd ever seen.

"Why, Miss Brady, I'm not following anyone. Lucky here just decided to walk along beside you." Clay shrugged while a half grin sat on his lips. "He's a smart horse. Knows a pretty woman when he sees one."

"Well, I wish you would just move on." Joanna started walking away as quickly as she could.

A little nudge had Lucky beside her again. "You aren't mad at me for some reason, are you?"

Joanna swung back to look at him. Stomped her foot. "Yes." With that one word, she started on again.

"Mind tellin' me what I did?" Clay raised his voice without moving forward.

She kept walking faster than before, but her voice reached him easily enough. "You got a black eye."

Clay stared at her retreating form for a second and then laughed aloud. He let her get almost to the next cross street before he nudged Lucky forward. If he died of old age, he would never understand a woman.

He didn't stop this time but rode slowly past with a wave and a smile. "I'll see you about ten in the morning, Miss Brady, at the library. Reckon I might as well see what you need done so I can get on it like I promised."

He didn't wait for her answer, but turned Lucky down the cross street and rode out of town.

ஃ

Joanna spent the first two hours after breakfast Monday morning debating. Should she go to the library or should she forget Clay Shepherd had returned to town?

Like she could do that. She collapsed into her favorite chair as her breath rushed out. What should she do? She had thought to ignore both Mark and Clay, but that didn't seem possible. Clay wouldn't let her.

She stood with a sigh. Maybe Carrie had a point. She'd prayed for excitement, and she'd gotten more than she expected. Now she might as well go face the answer to her prayer.

The warm summer sun shone down on Joanna as she walked across town. She purposely picked the path across the street from the feed store and was glad when she didn't see Mark. When she arrived at the little house that would soon become Cedar Bend's library, she saw Clay's horse grazing in the side yard. He lifted his head and whinnied at her when she opened the gate and started up the walk to the porch.

Joanna pushed the front door open and stepped inside. The cooler, stale air of the closed house greeted her. Then Clay stepped out of the kitchen with a grin on his face and a wooden ruler in his hand.

"Good morning, Miss Brady."

She clenched her jaw. "Why are you trying to irritate me?"

His dark brows rose. "Irritate you? What are you talking about? I've come to help you."

She resisted the urge to stomp her foot. She hadn't thrown a temper tantrum since she was a child, but lately she had come close more than once. Clay Shepherd had a knack for bringing out the worst in her. Now she folded her arms and lifted her chin. "You know exactly what I mean. Calling me 'Miss Brady' yesterday and today."

Mischief twinkled in Clay's eyes. He took a step closer to her. She felt crowded although half a room separated them. She couldn't look away from his eyes when the mischief faded, replaced by an intensity that frightened her.

He spoke in a soft voice. "I'd rather call you darlin'."

"No." She threw her hands out in a gesture to keep him away. "We shouldn't even be here alone like this. I don't know what I was thinking."

"Joanna, don't." Clay crossed the room before she could get the door open.

He didn't touch her, but he leaned against the door to block her escape. "Forgive me, please." She had never seen such a serious look on Clay's face, and it frightened her. "I didn't mean anything disrespectful. I'm sorry. I'm sorry for getting a black eye. And mostly I'm sorry for not bringing a chaperone today, because you tempt me more than any girl I've ever met. You always have. I never forgot you, Joanna."

His quick grin took her by surprise. "I never forgot the mistletoe, either."

Joanna's face flamed at the memory of her first and only

kiss. She would never forget that mistletoe. In fact, she still had it. That day long ago she had taken the green sprig and pressed it between the pages of one of her father's large medical books. She kept it in her treasure box tucked safely away in the drawer of her bedside table.

Clay stepped away from the door and motioned toward the opposite wall. "I assume you'll want some shelves here coming out into the room with one end attached to the wall. The libraries I've seen usually have shelves to the ceiling with a divider in the middle so you can put books on both sides."

"You've been to libraries?" This was a side of the wild, fun-loving cowboy that Joanna hadn't expected.

He shrugged. "Sure, ropin' and brandin' and bustin' wild broncs is a physically drainin' job. Nice to relax with a good book once in a while." He waggled his eyebrows at her. "You did know I can read, didn't you?"

Joanna giggled. "I seem to recall from our school days that you used to read fairly well."

Clay laughed. "Glad to know your memories don't exclude me."

Oh, if he only knew. Lord, I don't know what's happening here. Joanna breathed a prayer even as she recognized the serious meanings behind Clay's jokes. *Every time I'm with him, I become more entangled in my feelings for him. But I can't fall in love with him, Lord. I know he went to church yesterday, but I don't think he's a Christian. Mariah is right. I can't let myself love the wrong man. Please, Lord, bring Clay to salvation.*

thirteen

As soon as Joanna told him what she wanted done, Clay opened the door and told her he'd handle it from there. She walked back home feeling as if she'd just been sucked into a whirlwind and thrown back out.

The next few weeks were busy for Joanna as she met with the library committee and made plans for the upcoming rodeo and box supper at the Fourth of July community celebration.

For the most part, she kept her distance from both Mark and Clay, although she saw them in church. Mark tried to approach her several times, but she managed to either sidestep him or speak briefly and move on.

Clay seemed to be biding his time, or maybe he no longer cared. Joanna missed his admiring looks, as he seemed more interested in the pastor's sermons than he did in winning her affections. She knew she should be glad, because she had been praying for his salvation. And truly she was glad. In fact, encouraged by his apparent interest in spiritual things, she prayed even harder. But that didn't stop the longing deep in her heart for something she probably shouldn't have. After all, she felt as if the adventure she had prayed for had ended before it began.

❧

One evening in late June, several from the community and from the ranch met at the future library to work. As Joanna and her father arrived, she saw three farm wagons and another buggy stopped along the street. Mariah's cousin, Gladys Jacobs, called a greeting as she and her husband turned in at the gate.

Joanna and her father followed the Jacobses to the door. Gladys stopped to speak. "We couldn't be more proud of you, Joanna, for the work you are doing here."

"Thank you, Mrs. Jacobs." Joanna smiled. "But I'm not doing much. Everyone has pitched in to help. We wouldn't have a library without Mariah's generosity and her work."

At that moment Mariah appeared in the open door. She greeted her cousin with a hug then slipped an arm around Joanna. "Come on in. We couldn't wait to get started. I hope you don't mind."

"Of course I don't mind. That's less work for me." Joanna watched her father disappear around the corner of the house where some men were setting up a sawhorse. She wondered if Clay was there but decided it didn't matter. He probably wouldn't talk to her anyway.

Inside, Joanna spoke to Carrie and Lucille, Gladys's daughter. Both young married ladies were expecting, Carrie for the first time, Lucille with her second baby. They had been given the job of corralling the young children and were heading outdoors to play in the grass.

Hope grabbed Joanna for a quick hug as she passed. "I gots to help Carrie take care of my baby brohver. Bye. I love you."

With a quick wave, the little girl ran out the door almost before Joanna could respond. She and Mariah laughed.

"Oh, Joanna, there's someone I want you to meet," Mariah said. "I think she's in the kitchen."

Joanna stopped short when she saw Mark's broad back. He stood in the middle of the kitchen talking to someone and effectively hiding the person from Joanna's view.

"Mark, I hate to interrupt, but I'd like to introduce Liz to Joanna."

At Mariah's voice, Mark turned. His gaze caught and held Joanna's while a strange feeling swept through her. He looked—guilty.

He held out a hand, palm toward her. "I was just talking to Miss Cramer, honest."

The truth hit Joanna like a slap in the face. Mark did feel guilty. He looked like a little boy who'd been caught taking something that didn't belong to him. Joanna wanted to laugh and cry at the same time. Instead, she stepped into the room, eager to meet the woman who made Mark feel as if he needed to explain a simple conversation.

"Joanna, I'd like for you to meet Cedar Bend's new schoolteacher, Miss Elizabeth Cramer. I left the school-children of Cedar Bend high and dry when I married Mr. Butler." Mariah laughed. "We are glad to have a replacement arrive so early in the summer. Liz will have time to become acquainted before school begins this fall."

From the corner of her eye, Joanna watched Mark slink out the back door and wondered how a man so large could move so quickly without making a sound.

"Liz, this is Joanna Brady. Her father is our doctor, and Joanna is the librarian and our boss tonight."

Miss Cramer looked scarcely old enough to teach. She had large blue eyes and a halo of blond hair with loose curls that she wore tied back at the nape of her neck and falling to her waist. She stood at least two inches shorter than Joanna and a good ten pounds lighter. No wonder she had been hidden behind Mark. She wore a simple, everyday dress, and her smile seemed genuine as she extended her hand.

"Miss Brady, I have been hearing your praises since I arrived in town almost a week ago. I'm so glad to meet you." Liz gave Joanna's hand a firm shake before she glanced around the kitchen. "What you are doing is wonderful. Every town should have a library. The gift of reading is a precious thing that should be encouraged."

"Yes, I think so." Joanna felt tongue-tied in front of the nearly perfect schoolteacher.

"I hope we can become the best of friends." Liz smiled sweetly. "Cedar Bend is such a friendly town. Everyone I've met has been helpful. Mark"—her cheeks colored—"I mean Mr. Hopkins was the first to lend a helping hand. He happened by when I arrived and carried my trunk upstairs at the boardinghouse. I couldn't believe how easy it looked for him to carry such a heavy load."

"Is that right?" So that's why she hadn't seen Mark all week. "I'm sure he didn't mind. He enjoys helping."

"I guess you know him pretty well, then." Liz laughed. "But of course you do. This is a small town. You probably know everyone here."

"That's true, but Mark and I go way back. We've been friends forever." Joanna felt like the dog that looked into a pond at another dog with a bone. Wanting that new bone so much, he opened his mouth to steal it away and lost the one he had. Had she wanted Clay only because he was a new bone? He was exciting and dangerous just as she had prayed. He'd always been mysterious and unpredictable. Had she only wanted him because he seemed unattainable? Had she lost Mark when she should have kept him?

At that moment the back door opened and Clay walked in. Joanna's heart raced in a way that it never did around Mark.

He looked at her and grinned while all her doubts flew away. Clay was no reflection in a pond.

Mark followed Clay inside with several cut boards in his hands. His gaze flew first to Liz and then to Joanna. At that instant, she knew what she had thought all along. She loved Mark, but only as a friend.

She looked back at Clay and smiled. She had fallen in love with Clay when they were children in school. When he left, she had set that love aside to become a dream and a memory. Now that he had returned, her longings had been set free to become reality. No wonder she had wanted a man that was a tad dangerous and mysterious. Since her heart had longed for Clay all along, he was the one she had prayed for.

Suddenly her dreamworld crashed at her feet. She couldn't love Clay. Although he went to church, and she knew many were praying for him, he might never make a commitment to serve God.

"Hey, Joanna," Clay called to her. "Are you ladies going to paint that wall before we attach the shelving unit to it?"

"Yes, of course," Joanna answered and then looked to Mariah for guidance. "Do you know if they've already started on that?"

Mariah laughed. "I'm afraid we've been standing around gabbing while everyone else has been working. Let's go see what they've done."

While the ladies moved on to the next wall, Joanna held boards for Clay to secure together into shelves.

"Here, hold this one like this." Clay took Joanna's hands and placed them where he wanted her to hold the board.

At his touch, her blood stirred, but she kept her hands steady so he wouldn't guess how she felt.

Scarcely paying attention to the activity around her, Joanna helped Clay and listened to the account of his life at the Circle C. He seemed to like working on the ranch. "There're some mighty pretty spots out there. Maybe someday I'll take you out for a picnic."

Joanna tried to sound as if she didn't care. "That should be fun."

"Then we'll count on it." Clay gave her a quick smile that set her heart pounding.

When they finished putting a row of shelving together, Clay went outside and Joanna saw Mariah heading her way.

"So what's going on between you and Mark?" Mariah spoke with the bluntness of close friends.

"Mark?"

"Yes, Mark. I thought you two were pretty close not that long ago."

Joanna thought of Mark and the friendship they had shared for so many years. She said, "I guess you're right, Mariah. Something has happened. I always took for granted that Mark and I would marry someday. Now I don't think so. Actually, I wonder if he doesn't feel the same way. I've scarcely seen or spoken to him since the church social when he and Clay fought."

"Clay." Mariah repeated the name as if it left a bitter taste in her mouth. "I wonder if Sherman made a mistake in giving that young man a job."

"Why do you say that?" Joanna's eyes widened in surprise. Mariah always seemed to love everyone. Why would she pick on Clay?

"Because he isn't a Christian. Because his good looks and his wild reputation have turned my best friend's head." Mariah touched Joanna's arm. "Please, be careful in forming too close a friendship with him. Surely you know I want the best for you. I thought that was with Mark, who is a good, Christian man."

"Mariah, I would never marry a man who does not share my Christian beliefs." She gave a short laugh. "This is all hypothetical anyway. Clay has been a perfect gentleman and has never indicated any interest in a lasting alliance."

"I'm glad to hear that, Joanna." Mariah smiled. "Remember I am praying for you."

Joanna watched Mariah turn away to check on her children. She thought of Clay, and a smile touched her lips. She couldn't stop the warm glow that filled her heart when his image appeared in her mind. What would it hurt to be friends with him? Surely a few days of fun could not be wrong.

Joanna ignored the fact that Clay already held her love, and if he crooked his finger, she would be powerless to resist.

☙

As Clay went outside, he met Mark and Mr. Butler carrying a load of boards into the house. They said they would put them together, so he stepped over to the corner of the house where Lucas Nolan, the local sheriff, sat on an overturned bucket taking a break.

"Hey, Shepherd," Luke greeted him with a grin.

Clay nodded and asked, "Could you spare me a minute?"

"Sure, what's on your mind?"

Clay crouched down to sit on his heel. He picked up a pebble and tossed it back. "I've been seeing you in church every time I go, so I reckon you're no stranger to God."

Luke nodded. "We're on pretty good speakin' terms, yeah."

"I've been hearing some things." Clay gave a short laugh. "I mean they aren't exactly new ideas. I went to church when I lived here before, but I reckon I never understood about being saved. Isn't that what you all call gettin' right with God?"

Luke nodded.

Clay shrugged. "Looks like there oughta be more to it than just saying I'm sorry."

"You're right." Luke said. "Every one of us has sinned. I suppose you'd be lying if you said you didn't already know that."

Clay grinned. "That part I haven't had any problem understanding."

Luke chuckled. "Good, because that's the first step. Next you need to confess all your wrongdoings to the Lord."

As Luke talked, Clay listened without interruption. Finally, Luke said, "I reckon the bottom line, Clay, is this: Do you want to continue living your own way, which takes you down the road to destruction, or are you ready to accept God's salvation and the freedom to live for Him?"

"And spend eternity in heaven," Clay added. He looked down at the twig he had snapped into several pieces before he tossed them aside and stood. "Sounds like a big decision to me. Reckon something like that shouldn't be entered into without thinking it through. Thanks for talking to me."

"Don't think too long, Clay," Luke cautioned. "When Jesus knocks on your heart's door, that's the time to respond. Seems to me He's knocking now. Don't turn Him away."

Clay nodded. "I understand. I'll keep what you said in mind. Thanks, Luke."

With that, Clay went back inside the house.

fourteen

Cedar Bend's Fourth of July community celebration turned out even better than Joanna had expected. Surely everyone in town and for miles around had shown up. Horses grazed in the vacant lot across from the feed store where farm wagons, buggies, and a few surreys had been parked.

Booths selling crafts and homemade jellies and preserves were set up along either side of Main Street. The aroma of barbecue beef roasting over an open pit tempted the appetites of those who walked by.

Less than a block away, in the city park, several musicians had gathered in the bandstand to play rousing patriotic songs that could be heard all over town.

Since her father had been called out to tend to an injury, Joanna decided she would walk to town. Her father promised to meet her before noon so they could eat together. After he left, Joanna set off on foot. Now she walked past the busy booths while the band played and a dozen conversations sounded around her. She called out greetings to the men and women running the booths as well as the townsfolk who were spending money, making the day a success.

As she walked on, she sniffed the air appreciatively. The Circle C had pulled their chuck wagon in and set it up on the corner. A couple of tables and benches sat off to the side. A little old man wearing denim pants and a red plaid shirt bent over a couple of huge iron pots above an open fire, stirring first one and then the other.

"Hey, Mac," Joanna called to him.

He looked up with a welcoming grin on his leathery face. "Howdy, Miss Joanna. Got some books fer ya in the wagon."

"For me or for the library?" Joanna stepped closer and peered into one of the pots. "Mmmm, this looks as good as it smells."

Mac chuckled. "If you're hintin' fer a sample, cain't oblige. This here's fer barbecue beef sandwiches. The books in the wagon's fer you ta read. Put 'em in the library when yer done."

"Good." Joanna smiled at her friend and fellow romance book lover. She often traded books with Mac. He seemed to enjoy the stories as much as she did.

"Jist don't ferget ta git 'em before we leave here tonight," Mac cautioned her.

"Oh, don't worry. I won't. I'll be back for one of those sandwiches, too." She laughed. "I probably should pack a couple in a box for the supper this evening. That way I'd be assured of my box selling."

Mac gave her a sharp look. "I heard about them two fellers fightin' over you."

Joanna felt the color rise in her cheeks, but she shook her head. "I don't think so, Mac. They were fighting over some silly grudge from when they were boys. I don't think either of them even know what it was."

"Reckon they'll be biddin' on your box anyhow."

"Thanks, Mac, but it doesn't matter. I just want to raise a lot of money for the library. That's what's important."

Joanna watched Mac stir the beef before she moved on

down the street. She hadn't gone far when someone fell into step with her.

"Hi, Joanna."

She looked up into clear blue eyes and lost the ability to think. Finally, she remembered to answer. "Hi, Clay."

"I've been hearing some pretty nice comments about you."

"Really?"

"Yep. Makes me proud to be your friend." Clay looked down into Joanna's eyes. "We are friends, aren't we, Joanna?"

Friends. How could she resent such a nice word? But she didn't want to be friends with Clay. Not when there was so much more they could be to each other. Then Joanna's conscience pricked. Unless he accepted Christ's love and sacrifice as a free gift, they would have to remain only friends.

She nodded. "Yes, of course we are, Clay. Friends for life."

He looped her arm though his and grinned. "Good, then why don't you come with me to the park. Someone is getting ready to make a speech. A state representative, I think. Wonder how we rated his attention."

"It wasn't too hard." Joanna giggled. "He's the mayor's cousin."

After listening to the speech, visiting with the Butler family, and watching a ball game in progress, Clay and Joanna headed back toward Main Street where they met Dr. Brady.

"How's the little Johnson boy?" Joanna asked.

"He's fine. Just a sprained wrist when he jumped from a tree. His mother thought sure he'd broken his arm, but when I wrapped his wrist and told her he'd be fine, she bundled the kids into the wagon and came to town."

"Wonderful. Are you hungry, Dad?" Joanna glanced up at

Clay, who stood quietly behind her. "We were just thinking about those barbecue sandwiches Mac's got cooking. I've been smelling them all morning, and I'm about to starve."

"Is that right?" Dr. Brady seemed interested in something beyond his daughter. A quick smile touched his face. "I know we planned to eat together, but Clay's here and I see a friend. I believe I'll let you go ahead without me, if you don't mind."

As her father hurried off, Joanna turned to watch, but all she could see was Mrs. James with two of her children standing a few feet away. Surely he wouldn't. . .

"Clay, do you see that?"

Clay chuckled. "What's wrong, Joanna? Don't you think your father should have a lady friend? Are you jealous?"

"Of course not," Joanna protested. "I know they're friends. I've seen them talk at socials for the last year or so. My mother died about the same time Mr. James was killed in that accident. They have a lot in common I guess."

Clay laughed. "You know your father isn't ancient, don't you? What is he, about forty years old?"

She nodded. "Yes, he's forty-two."

"I always wished my pa would remarry. That was one of my dreams when I was a kid. But he never did. Said no one else could measure up to my ma. Maybe he was right." Clay took Joanna's hand. "Come on. Let's get something to eat. You aren't the only one who's starving."

After they ate, Clay and Joanna spent the afternoon together watching the contests in the park. Everything from prettiest baby to frog jumping had been planned.

She saw Mark a few times, but he never tried to speak to her. She didn't know whether to be glad or hurt. Once she saw him with the new schoolteacher. They seemed deep in conversation, and she wondered if anything might develop between the two of them. She remembered her prayer for someone to love Mark and offered another that if Liz was God's choice, Mark would be able to see her in the right way.

"I'm riding in the rodeo." Clay made the announcement as they sat on a park bench listening to a group sing gospel songs from the bandstand.

Joanna wanted to tell him he could get hurt riding a wild bronco, but somehow she knew he would just laugh at her. So she said nothing.

"That means I've got to go get ready." Clay shifted closer to her. "Will you watch me ride, Joanna?"

She nodded. "Of course I will."

Clay stood. "Come on. I'll walk you back to the Circle C's booth. I imagine Mariah and Carrie will be there since Luke is riding and the ranch is sponsoring the event."

Joanna let him hold her hand as they walked. It felt so right. They had spent almost the entire day together, and not once had she wanted to leave him. In fact, she found the thought of being separated from Clay during the rodeo almost unbearable. Of course, that was probably because of the danger involved. She tugged him to a stop as they neared the chuck wagon.

He looked down at her. "Something wrong?"

"No. . .yes. . .maybe."

Clay grinned. "Ain't nothin' like knowin' how you feel about something, is there?"

Joanna sighed. "That's the problem. I do know." She met his amused gaze with a frown. "I just don't want you to get hurt."

His chuckle did nothing to relieve her worries. He brushed a wisp of hair from her cheek and smiled at her as if he really cared. "Joanna, I've been riding a horse since I could sit in the saddle. I'd already broken my share of wild horses before you ever met me. This is something I do all the time."

"Do you mean you've never been hurt?"

"Now I didn't exactly say that." He grinned. "Don't reckon you need to worry, though, not with your pa there. I hear he's got the prettiest nurse west of the Mississippi to help him sometimes, too."

"Clay Shepherd!" Joanna stomped her foot. "If you get hurt I'll help him all right, and I'll make sure the cure is worse than the injury."

Clay laughed and gave Joanna a kiss on the forehead so quickly she wondered if she'd dreamed it. He turned her toward the corner. "You do that, darlin', and I'll come back every time a horse throws me just so I can watch your beautiful brown eyes shoot sparks at me."

A half hour later, Joanna sat with Mariah and Carrie to watch the rodeo. She saw her father walk past with Mrs. James. He listened to something she said and then laughed. An uneasy feeling twisted Joanna's stomach. Certainly her father was not old, but still, he didn't need to make a spectacle of himself in front of all their friends.

Then a rider shot through the gate and Joanna lost interest in her father. Glad that she scarcely knew the cowboy, who at that moment flew through the air and landed in the dust before rolling to his feet, she tried to relax. Clay stood inside the fence, his blue shirt and white Stetson easy to find. Of course, she figured she could pick him out of a line of identically dressed cowboys a thousand paces away without half trying. Her heart would lead her to him every time.

Several more riders hit the dust, but some stayed on the entire eight seconds, including Luke Nolan. Carrie whistled through her teeth when he walked away from his ride. The next cowboy didn't do as well.

"Too bad," Carrie said. "That one didn't stay on long."

"How do you stand it?" Joanna asked her friend. "When Luke rides, aren't you afraid for him?"

"Of course I am." Carrie rolled her eyes. "But this is nothing compared to the wild steer Luke rode before we were married. I think he was trying to impress me, although he won't admit it."

"Oh my." Joanna couldn't stop the image of Clay on the back of a wild longhorn steer. She thought horses were bad enough, but at least they didn't have horns and they generally stepped over the cowboy unlucky enough to land near their hooves.

Carrie smiled. "He was supposed to ride for five seconds, but he stayed on for ten before he jumped off. When I saw he was safe, I felt so weak I couldn't even stand up."

"Oh my." Joanna couldn't think of anything else to say even though her friends laughed at her. She turned back to watch and saw that Clay now sat on the back of a fidgeting horse in the chute. She saw him give a nod to the men surrounding him, and then the gate opened and the horse shot through.

Joanna watched the bronco lower his head and lift his back, twisting first one way and then the other while Clay held one gloved hand high and stayed with the horse as if he anticipated every move. Each second seemed an hour to

Joanna as she watched Clay ride. Then the whistle sounded and Clay jumped to the ground, running a few feet away with both hands raised in victory.

Those watching cheered, but no shouts were so heartfelt as Joanna's. She stood clapping while tears ran down her cheeks. Clay was safe. He had not been bucked off. He had not been trampled to death. She saw his wide grin and knew he felt good about his ride. He saw her and waved. She lifted her hand and waved at him, although what she really wanted to do was smack him for scaring her so much.

When the rodeo ended, Clay and Joanna walked to the city park where the bidding on the ladies' boxes would take place. They had spent a long day together, and the sun hung low in the western sky by the time they reached the park. If she could, Joanna would pull the sun back a few hours so her time with Clay wouldn't have to end so soon.

As the bidding started, one box after another found a home. Married women seldom had competition for their boxes. But several unmarried men bid the other boxes up to a hefty price.

As the new schoolteacher stepped forward, Joanna was surprised at the bids. But what surprised her even more was the fact that Mark Hopkins was one of the most energetic bidders.

Not sure how she felt about Mark's switch of affection from her to Elizabeth, she watched the bidding reach almost ten dollars before it stopped with Mark as the winner. Surely he had just spent every cent he had.

Clay chuckled and gave Joanna a hug while he spoke close to her ear. "Don't tell me you're jealous."

She jerked away just enough so he dropped his arm. "Of course not. Why would I be?"

"Can't think of a single reason." He took her arm and pulled her back next to him as he spoke for her ear alone. "You're a sight prettier than that little blond schoolteacher anyhow."

Joanna walked to the front and picked up her box with more confidence than she'd had when Liz's box brought so much. Even if Clay's bid was all she got, she wouldn't mind.

"Now here's the lady who got this box supper together for us. And that's not all. The profits go toward the new library Miss Brady is building for Cedar Bend." Karl Braun, serving as auctioneer, said, "Let's give Miss Brady a big hand for all the work she's done for our town."

If her confidence had faltered before, it soared now. Joanna couldn't stop smiling as her friends and neighbors stood and clapped. A few whistled and cheered. When someone called for a speech, the clapping faded into silence.

With the flush of embarrassment staining her cheeks, Joanna lifted her chin and said, "Thank you all so much, but I don't deserve your praise. Without each of you coming out and giving of yourself and your hard-earned money, today would have been wasted time. So many of you have put in more time and talent to make our celebration a success than I did. The Butlers, the Nolans, the Jacobses, Mrs. James, the Brauns. I shouldn't have started naming, because there are so many, but you all know."

She lifted her fingers to her lips and threw a kiss to everyone. "Thank you for today and for all the work you've already done on the library. And please remember that Cedar Bend's library is your library."

After that, Mr. Braun had more bids than he could keep up with. Joanna's box passed ten dollars, and she worried Clay wouldn't have enough. An easy smile sat on his face, so she figured he either had a pocket full of money or he didn't care if he lost. Then the bidding stopped with Clay's offer of eleven dollars and fifty cents.

Joanna spread her blue and white checked tablecloth on the grass, and Clay set her box in the middle. As they sank to either side to unpack their supper, Joanna said, "I'm afraid I didn't pack enough."

Clay grinned. "For my appetite or for my money?"

"Neither. I mean for the money you used to have."

His chuckle let her know he didn't mind. "Darlin', you're worth every penny."

fifteen

With their library money safely deposited in the bank, Joanna opened her home to the library committee one warm day in the second week of July. While their children played in the yard outside, several women crowded into the Bradys' parlor to look over some publishers' lists Mariah had received in the mail.

"We have enough money to get several books, don't we?" Gladys Jacobs asked.

Joanna nodded. "Yes, but we've already been accepting donations of used books. I've made a list of what we have to date. That way we won't duplicate when we order."

Mrs. James looked up with a smile for Joanna. "You've done a wonderful job, dear. How soon do you think the door will be open for business?"

After she had gotten over the shock of seeing her father with another woman, Joanna decided she liked his choice. Mrs. James never pushed her way on anyone, yet she was friendly and helpful. All four of her children were well behaved and seemed to accept the doctor as part of their family. Joanna had made the decision that she would accept the James family into their family just as graciously, if that was what her father wanted.

She smiled at Mrs. James. "Thank you. I'm not sure when we can open. Mariah, how soon do you think our new books will come once we order them?"

"I would allow at least a month." Mariah lifted her five-month-old baby son to her shoulder and patted his back. "We have to consider the time for the order to travel to the publishers, shipping time for the books, and processing of the orders."

"Wouldn't it be nice if the library could open about the same time school starts this fall?" Liz smiled. "That would give us even more to look forward to."

Mariah smiled at the young teacher. "I understand. I taught for many years, but not once did I approach the opening of school without a great deal of nervous anticipation."

Liz looked around the group and sighed. "Oh dear, here I sit with three of Cedar Bend's former teachers. I feel like such a novice. This is my first year to teach. I can only hope I will be able to fill your shoes."

Carrie and Lucille exchanged amused looks and giggles. Carrie reached over and patted Liz's hand. "Don't even try to fill mine. I only taught one year. If I did anything right, it was an accident."

"Me, too," Lucille said. "I'm only too glad to pass on the banner."

"Just be careful," Mariah added, "that you don't follow our examples. We each taught only one year here. My husband, who is on the school board, says Cedar Bend is destined to replace its teacher each year."

Carrie and Lucille giggled again before Carrie said, "What Mariah is saying, Liz, is that if you have any desire for marriage, you've come to the right place."

Liz's face turned an attractive shade of pink as she shook her head. "Oh no, I would never break my contract."

Mariah smiled. "That's all right, Liz. The contract is only for one year, and if what I saw on the Fourth of July is any indication, you've already caught the eye of several of our most eligible bachelors. Maybe one in particular."

Joanna watched Liz blush and deny that anything was going on between her and any of Cedar Bend's bachelors. She waited for the familiar feeling of loss and jealousy to hit her, and when it didn't, she knew she had completely given up Mark. She no longer felt as if he belonged to her. She no longer assumed that someday she and Mark would marry. Clay had taken that notion from her. And left her empty inside.

Feeling more than a little disgruntled, not because she had lost Mark, but because Clay was not hers either, Joanna said, "Maybe we should let our new schoolteacher mind her own romantic affairs while we pick out some books for our library."

As the women returned to the catalogs, Joanna noticed the concerned expression on Mariah's face before she looked away. When the other women left, Joanna would ask her friend to stay. She had to talk to someone before she made a complete mess of her life. Who better than her best friend?

ॐ

"Thank you for coming." When the last lady went out the door, Joanna turned to Mariah, the only one remaining. "I hope you didn't mind staying for a few minutes."

Mariah sat on the sofa. She leaned forward with her hands clasped in her lap. "Why do you suppose I sent Daniel and Hope home with Carrie? I'm not so insensitive that I can't see when my dear friend is hurting. Why don't you tell me what's troubling you?"

"Would you like some more tea first?" Joanna started toward the kitchen. Now that the time had come to confess, she just wanted to run away.

"Joanna." Mariah's voice was soft but firm. "Come and sit down. We'll have some tea later."

Retracing her steps, Joanna sank into her favorite chair near the sofa. "All right."

"Why don't you tell me what's troubling you? Does this have anything to do with the conversation we had with Liz? We were teasing her, but you know as well as I do that there is an element of truth in everything we said. I know you saw her with Mark on the Fourth of July and you couldn't have missed noticing they sat together in church last Sunday."

"I noticed." Joanna crossed her arms. Why she felt so cold in ninety-degree temperatures, she didn't know, but a chill moved through her body. "And I'm glad. I've been praying for Mark to find someone special. I think Liz is perfect. At first I thought she was too perfect to be real, but I like her. Really, I do."

"So you wouldn't mind if Liz takes over that house Mark was building for you?" Mariah's question sounded blunt to the point of being tactless, but Joanna knew she simply wanted a straight answer.

She shook her head, meeting Mariah's searching gaze with a steady one of her own. She tried to smile. "No, I honestly hope that is exactly what happens. Mark deserves someone as wonderful as Liz. I hope they do fall in love and get married."

Mariah sighed and leaned back against the sofa. "I assume that means your problems come from a different direction then."

"Yes." The word came out in a whisper. "I've done exactly what you told me not to."

When Mariah remained silent, Joanna looked at her and said, "When I was thirteen years old, Clay moved here with his father. Carrie said he was too wild, but I didn't think so. He became a symbol to me of everything romantic. He kissed me under the mistletoe, and I fell in love. With him or the idea of a boy actually kissing me, I don't know. I just know I loved him. Then he moved away. As the years passed, the memory I carried of Clay became my dream."

Mariah didn't move or speak.

"When I caught your wedding bouquet, Mark said we'd be next. That's when I prayed for God to send me someone exciting. I asked for an adventure, and God sent Clay. I assumed I'd marry Mark after my adventure ended, but I didn't know I'd fall in love again."

Mariah's intake of breath stopped her for a moment. Joanna wiped a drop of moisture from her eye. "I know. I shouldn't have. Carrie told me I needed to be careful. I didn't listen to either of you."

Joanna gave a short laugh. "Well, it's been an adventure, that's for sure. I think Clay is beginning to care for me. I've tried to just be friends, but I love him so much it hurts. He isn't a Christian. Oh, he goes to church, but that isn't enough. Mariah, what should I do?"

"Besides doing some serious praying, I think you know the answer to that, my dear friend." Mariah gave Joanna the hint of a smile.

Another tear slipped from Joanna's eye and she wiped it away with her finger. "I have to break off my friendship with

Clay, don't I? Mariah, will you pray with me?"

&

"Hey there." Clay fell into step with Joanna after Sunday morning service. His horse followed along behind while he held the reins. "Care if we walk with you?"

Her heart did a funny little flip before she could stop it. She shook her head. "No, of course not."

"Where's your pa?"

Joanna smiled. "He's taking someone home from church."

Clay gave her a searching look. "Reckon you got over that jealous streak."

"Jealous!" She threw him a disdainful look. "I was never jealous. I don't get jealous."

"So you wouldn't mind if Lucky and I take that pretty little schoolteacher for a ride out in the country this afternoon. Is that right?"

Skidding to a stop, Joanna stared at Clay. Surely he wasn't serious. "Together? On the same horse? There isn't room."

Clay laughed. "For the right woman I'd borrow Sherman's buckboard."

Joanna crossed her arms as her brows drew together. "And I suppose Liz Cramer is the right woman for you."

"I never said she was. I just said you were jealous." Clay's eyes danced in amusement.

"I am not."

"Methinks the lady doth protest too much."

"Oh!" Joanna's foot hit the dirt road, raising a puff of dust. "You are impossible."

"I know, but I'm still not taking Miss Cramer anywhere." Clay took Joanna's arm and headed her back down the road.

She lifted her chin. "I never thought you were."

"'Course not," Clay said. "Mark wouldn't let me."

Joanna met his teasing gaze and couldn't stop the laughter from bubbling. Even as she laughed, pain sliced through her heart. How could she ever give him up? She'd prayed with Mariah, but she hadn't been able to relinquish her feelings for Clay. She loved him and always would.

"Since I'm not giving the schoolteacher a ride this afternoon, how would you like to have a picnic?"

"A picnic?" Would it hurt to go on one last outing with him? Surely God had provided this time so she could tell Clay their friendship would have to come to a close. How she could possibly tell him without hurting his feelings, she didn't know, but she must try. She could not continue subjecting her heart to this torture of loving him yet knowing she could never be his.

"Yeah, there's a real pretty place I want to show you out on the Circle C. Tell you what," Clay said. "I'll borrow the buckboard from Sherman and have Mac pack a lunch from whatever he's got ready. Then I'll pick you up as soon as I can get back into town. How's that sound?"

As they crossed the yard to her house, Joanna smiled at Clay and nodded. "That sounds fine. Dad is eating at Mrs. James's today. I'll just leave him a note so he'll know where I am."

"Great." Clay's grin looked so happy Joanna felt like crying. What would he think if he knew what she planned to do? She'd eat one last meal with him and store away another wonderful memory, then probably break both their hearts when she told him she couldn't be his friend anymore because she loved him too much. He wouldn't understand, and she didn't blame him. How could he when she scarcely understood herself?

☙

Clay watched Joanna run up the porch steps and disappear inside her father's house. If he'd been a little quicker, he'd have given her a kiss to take with her. He turned and patted Lucky's neck before swinging into the saddle.

"Reckon the kissin' can wait." He headed toward the ranch, whistling the tune to a song they'd been singing in church that morning.

"She's the woman for me, Lucky. What do you think? Will she say yes when I ask her?"

Lucky answered with a whinny and a nod of his head.

Clay laughed. "Glad you agree, because if I can convince Miss Joanna Brady that I'm a good catch, she'll soon be part of our family."

A smile sat on Clay's face as he thought of Joanna. He loved her wide brown eyes that shot sparks at him when she was angry. For the last month, he'd been holding a tight rein just to keep his hands from touching her thick dark hair when she wore it down her back. Her smooth olive skin and full rosy lips were a temptation he could scarcely resist. Just holding her hand sent his blood pulsing through his body, but he hadn't fallen in love with her because she was beautiful.

Truth be told, there were plenty of beautiful women around, but none who possessed the inner beauty Joanna had. The woman he loved had strength of character. She wouldn't let anyone run over her, yet she freely gave of herself to the entire community. Her work for the library proved that if helping her father on his rounds didn't. Besides, she represented the stability he craved. He wanted to settle down right here in Cedar Bend, and he wanted to spend the rest of his life with Joanna by his side.

Clay gave Lucky his head as he picked up speed at the outer edge of town. Settling into an easy run for the big horse, they headed home.

sixteen

Joanna wrote a note for her father telling him she would be with Clay on a picnic at the Circle C. With her heart heavy, she went into her bedroom and changed into an everyday dress. Then she walked past the mirror and stopped. Reaching for her brush, she loosened the bun at the back of her head and brushed her long hair. Bringing the thick mass to the nape of her neck, she secured it with a ribbon, letting it hang free down her back. She washed her face and patted it dry.

Joanna walked into the parlor and sat in her favorite chair. Her Bible lay on the table beside the chair where she had dropped it when she came in earlier. She picked it up and ran her hand over the leather cover. She had been neglecting her Bible reading all summer.

Holding the book in her lap, Joanna opened the cover, letting the pages fall open near the middle. Psalms, without doubt, was her favorite book of the Bible. She glanced down and began to read from the thirty-seventh chapter. "Fret not thyself because of evildoers..."

She read through the third and fourth verses and then read them again, "Trust in the Lord, and do good; so shalt thou dwell in the land, and verily thou shalt be fed. Delight thyself also in the Lord; and he shall give thee the desires of thine heart."

Then the fifth and sixth verses said, "Commit thy way unto the Lord; trust also in him; and he shall bring it to pass. And he shall bring forth thy righteousness as the light, and thy judgment as the noonday."

Joanna looked up, letting God's promises speak to her heart as conviction rushed in. She had wanted the desires of her heart without trusting in the Lord to bring them to pass. When was the last time she had delighted herself in the Lord? No wonder Clay had not accepted salvation as she'd prayed. She had not set a godly example before him. Her righteousness had not been brought forth.

"Lord, please forgive me." Tears filled Joanna's eyes as she cried out in a heartfelt prayer of remorse that started her on the journey back to a right relationship with her Savior.

❧

"Can you smell that chicken?" Clay grinned at Joanna as she sat beside him on the buckboard seat. He flicked the reins, and the horses picked up the pace.

She sniffed the air and smiled. "Yes, Mac makes the best fried chicken of anyone I know."

Clay chuckled. "Mac can cook, that's for sure. I've never eaten so well. Makes a man want to stay around." He flashed her another grin. "Maybe settle down."

Joanna sucked in her breath, unsure if special meaning lurked behind his words and ready grin. She tried to smile. "That would be nice, Clay. I mean, everyone should have a place to call home."

She thought of the verses she'd just read. As the scripture said, she would wait upon the Lord and rest in Him. Surely He would bring His will to pass. But right now she wanted to enjoy the picnic with Clay, to store up memories for later.

As they turned toward the Circle C, Joanna relaxed. She and Clay talked about the perfect summer day, the wildflowers growing beside the road and scattered across the fenced-in fields on either side. They even talked about the cattle grazing some distance away on a slight rise.

"I'd like to have a spread of my own someday." Clay turned the buckboard onto a side road and looked out over the vast land before them as the horses moved forward. He chuckled. "Not necessarily this big. Actually, I wouldn't mind starting off with a small farm. I just want something of my own."

When Joanna only smiled at him, he veered off the road and pointed toward the distant hill. "Over that rise the land slopes down to one of the prettiest spots you'll ever see. There's a natural stream flowing through a stand of timber. The grass is thick and green, and at one place the bank runs right down almost level with the water. We should be able to find a bit of shade for our picnic."

"It sounds wonderful." For Clay's sake, Joanna wanted to be happy, to laugh and talk as if she didn't have a care in the world, but she couldn't.

He reached over and took her hand. "You're mighty quiet today. Got a lot on your mind?"

She nodded.

He grinned. "Me, too."

He gave her hand a gentle squeeze and then drove over the rise. As the buckboard lumbered down the hill, Joanna saw a dense stand of trees that seemed to go on to the horizon. Since they followed a meandering line about a hundred yards wide, she assumed the stream of water Clay had mentioned would be somewhere in the middle of the trees.

Clay brought the buckboard to a halt at the edge of the woods. "Sorry, but we'll have to hike to that pretty spot I told you about."

Joanna smiled at him. "I don't mind. I like to walk."

She wondered if she would be walking home after she told him what was on her mind.

Clay unhitched the horses and tied them so they wouldn't wander. He lifted Joanna from the buckboard and then pulled out the picnic basket. Holding the basket in one hand, he linked the fingers of his other hand through Joanna's, and they entered the cooling shade.

As they walked, Joanna noticed the trees were not so close together as she had thought, but were just far enough apart to create a comfortable setting. A breeze stirred, ruffling her hair and cooling her face. Their footfalls made a crunching sound, and the scent of pine lingered as they passed an evergreen tree. Birds chirped in the tops of the trees, and small animals scurried away from them.

In a small clearing, Joanna saw what Clay meant by the prettiest place she would ever see. A cleared patch of grass gradually sloped to the clear, blue-tinted water. She stopped. "Oh, Clay, you're right. It is beautiful."

He grinned as if he had ordered the spot just for her. "I knew you'd like it."

"I do. Thank you for bringing me here." If only she didn't feel like crying. If only she could forget what she had to say.

Clay set the basket down then lifted a large tablecloth from the top and started to unfold it. Joanna took the cloth from him. "That's my job."

She shook the cloth open, and it billowed out in the breeze before settling down on the grass. She sank to one side and looked at Clay. "Is this all right?"

His gaze never strayed from her face. The intensity in his eyes held her motionless. Then he smiled, and she breathed again. He answered, "It's perfect."

Clay sat beside her and put the basket between them. He took both her hands in his and said, "Will you pray before we eat? I'm not on the best speaking terms with the Almighty."

Which was exactly the problem. She wanted to yell at him, tell him he had to become a Christian. Because if he didn't, she couldn't go on any more picnics with him. She had already lost her heart to him; she was determined not to lose her faith, too.

Instead, she bowed her head and offered a short prayer of thanksgiving for food that she knew she probably wouldn't taste. Mac McDougal was considered one of the best cooks in the county, and the fried chicken he'd packed for Clay proved his expertise. On some level, Joanna knew the chicken and mashed potatoes tasted wonderful, yet they might as well have been cooked by her father, who thought boiling water was beyond him. Clay kept up the conversation, and Joanna contributed as much as she could.

Finally, Clay put his plate back in the basket and took Joanna's from her.

"Joanna, I've got something—"

"Clay, I need to—"

They both started and stopped at the same time. "You go ahead," Joanna said, glad for a reprieve.

Clay set her plate in the basket. He turned and, taking

both her hands in his, looked into her eyes with a serious expression. When Clay got serious, Joanna got nervous.

"Joanna Brady, I love you."

"Oh, Clay." She tried to pull her hands away, but he wouldn't let her.

"No, please, hear me out." She saw the love in his eyes, and she couldn't move because she loved him, too.

"I guess I fell in love with you when we were kids. I didn't know what it was then, but I know now. Joanna, will you marry me? I don't have much, but I can support a wife. Please say yes."

"Now ain't that the purtiest proposal ya ever did hear?" The man's gravelly voice and rough appearance as he stepped from behind a tree several feet away would have been enough to frighten Joanna, but the gun he pointed at Clay tore a scream from her lips.

&

"Mr. Simms." Clay stood quickly, placing himself between the man and Joanna. "I'm surprised to see you this far south."

"I reckon you are." The man spit a stream of tobacco juice to the side. "Thought you'd run out on us and never see us again, didn't ya?"

"I can't imagine what you are talking about." Clay held his hands out to the sides, hoping the outlaw he'd left in Nebraska wouldn't shoot an unarmed man. He took a few steps to the side. If possible, he might draw the man's attention away from Joanna.

"Even you ain't that stupid." Simms waved the gun. "One shot. That was the signal. Remember? Ya done asked, and I told ya twice. Where'd ya go when ya heard the signal? Ya run out on us, that's what ya done."

"I didn't run out on you, Mr. Simms." Clay shifted again. He hadn't run out; he'd let Lucky walk out of town. "I heard that first shot. Really I did. Then there were so many, I didn't know what had happened. You know, those horses you picked weren't real good for a bank job."

"What d'ya mean by that?" Simms swayed, and Clay figured he'd been drinking.

Clay took a step to the side. "All I'm sayin' is that those horses took off in three different directions with all that shootin' goin' on. With you not there to tell me what to do, I figured you'd want me to go after the horses. Never did catch 'em, though."

"Stand still." Simms growled at Clay. He lifted his gun so it again pointed at Clay's chest in a sort of wavering circle. As unsteady as Simms seemed, Clay feared he might aim at him and still hit Joanna.

"Yes, sir, Mr. Simms." Clay shifted again.

"Them two boys with us didn't make it. I got taken in. Spent a month in jail before I got away. Been trackin' you ever since. Gonna make ya pay fer what ya did."

"Mr. Simms, even if the horses hadn't run off, I couldn't have helped much. That place was crawlin' with the law. Don't reckon we had much of a chance anyhow."

"Don't matter. Ya run out on us. And yore gonna pay." Simms grasped his gun with both hands.

Clay glanced at Joanna. She sat where he'd left her, watching with large, frightened eyes. If he had to die, he wanted to save her. That's all that mattered.

"Don't ya move no more. I'm done talkin'."

Clay heard the click of Simms's gun being cocked, and he froze in place.

Joanna's scream and warning came in rapid succession. "Clay, look out."

Clay tried to turn, but he never saw what hit him as the crack of impact against his skull sounded at the same time pain exploded in his head. He crumpled to the ground.

seventeen

Joanna sat on the tablecloth transfixed, unable to move. She watched the man who had hit Clay with the butt of his six-shooter kneel and put a finger to Clay's neck. He then looked up at Simms with a grin. "Hit a man too hard one time. He never got back up. This one's fine, though."

"He better be." Simms growled and holstered his gun. "I didn't come all this way so's you could kill 'im. Well, tie 'im up, Burton. What ya waitin' fer?"

Joanna wanted to scream. She wanted to cry. Mostly she wanted Clay to get up, hold her close, and tell her it was all a bad dream. But Clay lay in a crumpled heap on the ground. She watched the man called Burton roll Clay over and tie his hands behind him. Next he tied his feet together, and then the two men lifted Clay into a sitting position and leaned him back against a tree, tying him in place.

Simms placed a big dirty boot on Mac's clean tablecloth, and before Joanna knew what he had in mind, he grabbed her by the arm and hauled her to her feet. She jerked and twisted, trying to get away from him, but he just laughed and tightened his grip.

"What are you doing? Let me go." She tried to stomp on his foot and missed. He wrapped an arm around her and held her against his filthy shirt. She gagged at the smell of sweat, horse, and liquor that radiated from Simms's body.

143

"Settle down, sister. You're comin' with us." She saw Burton dip his hat in the creek and toss water on Clay as Simms dragged her across the clearing.

He stopped by the tree where he had hidden earlier and, holding Joanna in front of him, sneered at Clay, who was coming around. "Hey, Shepherd, I'm takin' yer girl. Hope ya don't mind. You come and get her if ya want her."

His cruel laughter grated on Joanna's already raw nerves. "I promise I won't kill her till you show up. That is, iffn ya want her back and iffn ya can find us. I figure the two of you 'bout evens the score fer them two boys you let get killed."

As Simms tugged her around the tree, Joanna saw Clay jerk against the ropes binding him, and she knew he had regained consciousness.

Clay yelled, "Let her go, Simms. This ain't her fight. Why don't you face me like a man?"

Simms just laughed again and pulled Joanna with him. By the time they reached Simms's horse tied to a sapling, Joanna felt as if she had already prayed more than she had all summer. Her heart pounded, and she looked around, desperate for a means of escape. But even her struggles as the big man lifted her to the back of his horse did no good. He mounted behind her and, keeping a good hold around her waist, headed out. As they broke out of the trees and started across the prairie, Burton caught up. They rode for a while before they finally reined in and stopped on a small rise where they could see for miles in all directions.

"We're stoppin' here." Simms climbed down and dragged Joanna with him.

She stumbled to gain her balance on muscles weak with

fear and prayed silently. *Lord, please save me. Let someone find Clay and help him. Forgive me. I didn't know this would happen when I prayed for an adventure. I almost got Clay killed.*

As she realized what she was praying, the blood drained from her face. *Oh, Lord, they are going to kill us, aren't they? Both me and Clay when he comes after them. Please confound our enemies.*

The verses she had read in Psalms came back to her mind. *Fret not thyself because of evildoers.* Of course, that might be easier said than done, but she could try.

Simms gave her a shove. "Sit over there and don't try anything." He stuck his gun under her nose. "Your days were numbered the minute you hooked up with that yellow-livered Shepherd. Reckon ya know I'm gonna shoot ya first so's he can watch. Then I'm gonna shoot him."

Burton started toward Joanna. "If ya need her watched, I wouldn't mind at all." His leering expression left little doubt to his intentions.

"Get yourself away from her. She's bait and that's all." Simms dug a bottle out of his saddlebag and popped the cork. He took a long drink before handing it to the other man. "Here, take a swig of this. It'll calm yer nerves."

"I ain't nervous." Burton took the bottle and tipped it up then wiped his mouth with his sleeve. "I told ya when I took this job, I could kill a man easy as anyone."

He might not be nervous, but Joanna couldn't seem to keep her hands from trembling, and his bragging didn't help. She sank to the grass when her legs wouldn't hold her. She bowed her head and closed her eyes. *Lord, I know I've done a foolish thing. I love Clay, but he's not mine to love. For all these years I've remembered his wild, free spirit and thought of him as my hero. In all the books I've read, Clay became the dashing, exciting hero who won the maiden's heart. I thought that was what I wanted. I didn't know it would be like this, but You knew, didn't You?*

Tears filled Joanna's eyes as she thought of Clay. He didn't know the Lord. If he died because of her foolishness, he would die without Christ. She prayed for him, that he wouldn't come, although she didn't understand why the men thought he would after they'd tied him to a tree. The prayer she had prayed before she left home that afternoon had brought her closer to the Lord. She prayed now for forgiveness, for putting her desires above God's best for her and Clay.

Lord, please deliver us from this evil. Bring Clay to You so he will know the joy of Your salvation and have the promise of a home in heaven one day. And please forgive me for my discontent. Just, please Lord, save us and let us stay safe from now on, even if our lives are boring.

୬

Clay struggled against the ropes holding him as he watched Simms drag Joanna through the trees. He saw her fighting the big man and worried that she might be hurt. Then the trees blocked them from his view. When he heard the sound of hoofbeats going away, he knew they had taken her with them.

He renewed his efforts to free himself and found the rope went around his hands in a way that he could pull one hand back if he didn't struggle. With one hand free, he easily slipped the rope off his other hand and untied his feet. Obviously the man who tied him didn't know what he was doing.

On the other hand, maybe they intended for him to get

free after they had a head start. He knew Simms had been drinking, so he probably hadn't been thinking clearly, but why didn't he just kill him while he had the advantage? After all, he knew Clay wasn't armed. Why take Joanna and give Clay a chance to get his guns and track him down? It didn't make sense, but then he didn't figure Simms ever made much sense.

Clay stood and waited for his head to clear before heading toward the horses he'd left tied at the edge of the trees with the buckboard. Whoever hit him had left a knot the size of a walnut on the back of his head and a throbbing pain to boot. He untied one of the horses and hoisted himself on bareback. His instinct was to head after Simms, and he figured Simms was counting on that, but he had no weapon and no plan. He'd have to get some help.

Turning the horse toward the ranch house, Clay pushed the plodding animal into a run for Joanna's life. When he reached the house, he jumped from the horse and ran to the back door. Concern for Joanna took the place of his manners as he pulled the door open and stepped inside.

"Mr. Butler!" he called from the empty kitchen. Surely someone was here. "I need help!"

"In here." He heard Sherman's voice and followed the sound. The tall, broad-shouldered man met him just outside the parlor door, a concerned look on his face. "Clay, what's happened?"

"Joanna's been kidnapped."

"Joanna Brady?" The doorway filled as Mariah, Carrie, and Luke Nolan joined Sherman.

"Yes." Clay briefly explained Simms forcing him to hold

the horses while the three men robbed the bank in Nebraska. Then he said, "I'm to blame for this. I should have known my past would catch up with me. They won't touch her until they have me, but I'm afraid they plan to kill Joanna, too. Please, help me get her back to safety. Then when she's safe, if I'm still alive, I promise I'll ride out of her life and she'll never see me again."

"Don't worry, we'll get her back." Luke Nolan stepped into the hallway with Sherman. "Sherm, we need to round up a posse. How about some of your boys? Think they'd ride out with us?"

"Sure thing." Sherman nodded. "I'll go get Cyrus to tell the boys." He stopped long enough to place a fatherly hand on Clay's shoulder. "We'll get Joanna out of this. Just do whatever Luke says. He rode with the Texas Rangers, and he knows what he's doing. Later we'll talk about this notion of you running away. Best thing to do with your past is to face it head on."

Clay didn't answer as he followed the two men from the house. He ran to the bunkhouse and strapped on his six-shooters, grabbed his rifle, and made sure all the guns were loaded.

Cyrus soon created a stir among the cowboys as they came in and armed themselves in like manner. For the first time since he saw Bob Simms step from behind that tree, Clay felt as if Joanna might be safe. He didn't care so much about his own life, but he didn't want anything to happen to her.

eighteen

Twelve men gathered outside the bunkhouse and formed a semicircle around their boss. Sherman Butler explained the situation.

Then he said, "Men, you all know Joanna Brady. Clay says this outlaw has little respect for anyone, including women. He says he's pretty sure the man was drinking, and there's at least one more man with him, maybe a hired killer. The situation doesn't look good, but we know Someone who cares and is able to confound the evil deeds of such men. Let's go to Him now and ask for His help."

Clay watched the men bow their heads before he followed their example. As Sherman led a prayer for Joanna's safe rescue and their successful capture of the outlaws who had taken her, Clay felt a presence of comfort sweep over them.

Please, don't let them hurt her. Although he didn't speak aloud, he added his request to the others. From the moment he watched Simms drag Joanna away, Clay had been pleading in his heart for her safety. Whether he prayed or only gave words to his fears, he didn't know. But now, as he again pleaded for Joanna, he felt as if Someone might be listening.

Sherman brought the prayer to a close and waited while Luke looked around at the men, saying, "I can't promise your safety. We are dealing with outlaws who more than likely live by the gun and would kill as quick as they'd look at a man. If anyone wants to back out, not a word will be said."

He waited while the men either voiced their determination to bring Joanna back or simply stood with a nod and a stubborn expression.

"All right, men. Let's ride then." Luke gave the order for them to mount up.

Clay rode Lucky between Sherman and Luke. The rest of the men rode behind and to the side of them. They were all regular churchgoers and knew Joanna. Most had told Clay they would get her back and make sure Simms went to prison for a long time. They seemed to like and respect Joanna. Clay figured they had volunteered to go for her sake rather than for his, but he didn't mind. The important thing was that she be rescued from the lowlife who had taken her.

Clay pointed out the direction Simms had gone, and they soon found the trail easy to follow through the tall dry grass. After a few miles, Luke lifted his binoculars. He held up his hand as a signal to stop.

"There they are." He pointed to a distant rise where Clay could see dark spots against the background of brown and green grass.

Luke laughed. "They are sitting out in the middle of an open prairie without cover. Did they expect you to come after them alone?"

Clay nodded. "I never said Simms was smart."

"We can't take them by surprise. Not from where they are." Luke shrugged. "A full frontal approach is our only choice. Does that sound all right to you, Sherm?"

Sherman nodded. "Looks like the only thing we can do."

"We'd better spread out then." Luke turned to give orders

to the others. "We're going to ride straight on, and I want plenty of space between every horse. Those on the ends go ahead a few paces so we form a large semicircle around them. They may try to run when they realize Clay hasn't come alone, so be prepared to give chase. I want those men brought in. Unless I missed someone, there are only two men. Let's go get them."

Clay would have liked to surprise Simms, but he knew Luke was right. They had to approach the outlaws in clear view. If he saw so many riding toward him, would he kill Joanna?

Please, Lord, keep Joanna from harm.

This time Clay knew he had prayed, and he sure hoped God was listening. He nudged Lucky into line near the center of the semicircle and rested his hand on the gun at his side. With Luke's order to follow his lead ringing in his ears, Clay leaned low in the saddle and guided Lucky to run straight toward Simms.

❧

Joanna sat on the ground praying just as she'd been doing for what seemed like hours. Simms and Burton sat a few feet away, watching her and sharing their second round of liquor. She felt as bound as if she had ropes around her hands and feet because she knew they would catch her if she tried to get away.

After a while, Burton lay back and appeared to be asleep. Joanna prayed Simms would do the same, although she didn't know how anyone could sleep as hot as it was. The afternoon sun beat down on them without mercy, causing prickles of sweat to run down Joanna's back and neck. The grass under her scratched, and she shifted.

Simms had leaned back with his eyes closed but at her movement mumbled, "Jist sit still, girl. Your boyfriend'll come for ya soon enough. And then we'll put ya both ta sleep."

She cringed at the cruelty in his laugh and looked away. That's when she saw a dark line that seemed to stretch clear across the horizon. She glanced at the men. Both appeared to be sleeping. She prayed they were. Because, if she wasn't dreaming, that rapidly approaching line of horses meant help was on the way. She prayed the vibration of the horses' hooves against the ground would not alert the outlaws.

The riders were close enough for Joanna to recognize Clay on Lucky near the center of the line when she heard Simms let out a stream of cursing.

"Get up ya lazy, no good—"

Joanna scrambled to her feet, and so did Burton. She tried to ignore the filthy language coming from the two men as she whispered over and over, "Thank you, Jesus."

Then Simms grabbed her, jerking her in front of him like a shield. "Get a gun and start shootin'," he yelled at Burton.

"You stay and get yourself killed. I didn't hire on to fight an army." Burton jumped on his horse and took off. A man from either end of the line broke away and gave chase.

Her rescuers stopped in a circle that had Simms covered on all sides. Clay nudged his horse forward another step. "Let her go, Simms. You haven't got a chance."

Joanna felt the cold, hard metal of Simms's gun as he pressed it into her side. His laughter sounded crazed against her ear. "Not so fast, Shepherd. I got my ticket out of here. You let me go or she dies now."

"If you hurt her, you'll be a dead man, Simms. Take a look. You're surrounded." Clay nodded toward Luke. "The sheriff is here. Let her go and you'll get a fair trial."

"I ain't goin' back ta jail. Now let me out of here."

"Turn her loose, Simms."

"Do I look stupid?" The big man twisted to look from side to side, keeping Joanna against him. "Soon as I let her go, you'll shoot me."

"No we won't, Simms." Luke held his hand up and spoke to the other riders, "No one fires if he lets her go." Then Luke said, "It might interest you to know that some of the best shots in Kansas have you in their sights right now. Every one of them knows and respects Miss Brady, and they intend for her to leave here unharmed. They are just waiting for my signal. If you don't let the lady go, I'll let them cut you down."

Joanna felt the gun that was pressed into her ribs move. She held her breath, not knowing what Simms might do. She knew he was scared. So was she.

"Put the gun down, Simms," Clay ordered.

But he didn't. The outlaw lifted his gun and pointed it straight at Clay. "If I go, I'm takin' ya with me, Shepherd."

She'd been afraid before. Now she felt anger rise to push the fear aside. How dare this horrible man threaten Clay! He wouldn't get away with shooting the man she loved if she could help it.

Joanna sank the heel of her shoe into the arch of Simms's foot with as much force as she could muster. At the same time she leaned forward slightly to give more power to the jab of her elbow in his ribs. As she straightened, she felt the back of her head make contact with what she assumed was Simms's nose. Purely an accident, but not one she regretted.

Joanna heard the boom of the outlaw's gun go off as he howled and released her. She sank to the ground and curled into a ball, afraid to look.

A few more shots rang out, and then all was quiet.

"Clay's been hit."

Joanna heard Mr. Butler's voice above the others that called out orders as they took Simms into custody. She ignored the outlaw screaming words she didn't want to hear. She scrambled to her feet and pushed past those who stood between her and Clay.

He lay on the ground, his eyes closed in a face as white as the cuff on her sleeve. A crimson stream poured from the wound in his head. "No–o–o." Her cry became a wail. "Don't die, Clay. Please, don't die."

Cyrus knelt on the other side. He placed a folded white handkerchief on the blood and pressed. "He ain't dead, Joanna. Just knocked out."

When she only looked at him, not understanding, he went on in a calming voice. "Reckon you saved his life. I saw what ya done. Stompin' that feller's foot and bashin' his nose is what kept him from shootin' our boy here down."

"But he did get shot." She held Clay's limp hand in hers while tears ran down her cheeks. "I don't want him to die. Cyrus, please, don't let him die."

Cyrus chuckled. "Thought you was the nurse 'round these parts, Miss Joanna. Ain't you never seen a flesh wound before?" He lifted the blood-soaked handkerchief. "See here? Clay got his hat knocked off and his hair parted, that's all. The bleedin's already slowin' down."

"But he's unconscious."

Cyrus grinned. "Not for long, he ain't. He's comin' 'round now."

Joanna scarcely noticed the commotion around them as she watched Clay's eyes flutter open while color returned to his cheeks. She knew some of the men rode off, but she didn't bother looking up. Instead, she watched Clay's eyes widen and rest on her face. A faint smile touched his lips, and the strength returned in his hand as he squeezed her fingers.

"Are you an angel?"

At first Joanna thought his whispered question came from a fuzzy mind. Then Cyrus laughed and said, "Reckon our boy here thinks he's died and gone to heaven."

Clay's grin widened. "Anywhere Joanna is would be heaven."

Cyrus patted Clay's shoulder. "You'll be all right. Feel like sittin' up?"

"Yeah." Clay didn't take his gaze from Joanna as she helped Cyrus raise him into a sitting position.

Clay rested his arms across his knees and looked at Cyrus. "What hit me this time?"

"Just a little ole bullet." Cyrus picked up Clay's hat and handed it to him. "You might want to go bareheaded for a couple of days. Doc Brady should take a look at that and the knot on the back of your head soon as we can get ya to town. He'll give ya something for that headache. His nurse is too shook up to be much help."

Clay grinned at Joanna. "Sure am glad to see you're still breathing. Don't reckon Simms expected you to fight him. Last thing I saw was you stomping his foot."

He looked around with a frown. "What happened to Simms anyway?"

"Luke and some of the boys are takin' him in. They got the other fellow, too." Sherman stopped beside them and looked down at Clay. "That was a close one. I believe we owe the Lord a big thank you for saving your life. He and Miss Joanna here." He smiled at her. "Joanna, it took courage for you to do what you did. God answered our prayers and saved not only your life, but Clay's as well. Why don't we thank Him now?"

Clay struggled to stand, so Cyrus and Sherman helped him. Joanna let him take her hand in his and watched him bow his head while Sherman prayed. She felt as if her heart might break. How could she give Clay up now? Surely the Lord asked too much of her.

nineteen

Clay couldn't remember ever having such a headache. He clung to Lucky on the way back and fought the nausea rolling in his stomach. Any other horse might have dumped him, but Lucky stepped carefully as if he knew his master could scarcely hang on.

Joanna rode double with Mr. Butler to one side of Clay while Cyrus stayed abreast on the other side. Clay knew they kept a close watch on him, probably expecting him to fall off his horse. By the time they finally rode into the yard at the ranch, he felt so tired he could scarcely slide from Lucky. He desperately wanted to crawl into his bunk and sink into a sleep free of pain. But even more than that he wanted to see that Joanna got home safely.

Carrie ran out of the house with little Hope following. Mariah came right behind them with her son in her arms. "Joanna, are you all right?"

"I'm fine." She hugged them all and picked Hope up to hold her close. After assuring the little girl the bad man hadn't hurt her, she told her friends, "But Clay's been shot."

"Shot?" Mariah swung to look at him.

He held to Lucky's reins, letting his horse hold him upright, and forced a grin. "Nothin' to worry about, ma'am. Just got my hat knocked off."

"Oh my." Mariah turned back to her husband. "Sherman,

Clay needs to see a doctor. The men rode through here several minutes ago. Did they take those outlaws in? Did they get all of them?"

Mr. Butler slipped an arm around Mariah and held her close as he told her what had happened. Clay felt a pang of envy for the love that seemed to pass between the two of them. He'd give everything he had if he could experience that sort of love with Joanna. But this encounter with Simms had taught him a valuable lesson. Joanna didn't belong with him.

He scarcely listened to the others talk as he watched Joanna with Hope and knew his time with her was coming to a close. As soon as he felt well enough, he'd be moving on to Texas just as he'd planned. He couldn't stay around and endanger her life again.

His gaze shifted to his little buddy who had grown so much in the short time they'd been in Cedar Bend. Maybe he'd done something worthwhile by coming here, at least. Little Daniel had a good home with a loving family. He wouldn't have to grow up without a mother's love. Mr. and Mrs. Butler were the best parents any little fellow could hope for.

A jingle of harness and creaking of wood announced the arrival of the buckboard that Clay had borrowed. One of the ranch hands drove it around to the barn and through the wide-open doors. Clay was glad to see it had been returned without damage. Another man drove the family buggy and stopped beside the Butlers.

"We'd better get Joanna home and have Tom Brady take a look at you," Mr. Butler said to Clay. "Why don't we let Ben take care of your horse so you can ride with us?"

Clay knew Lucky wouldn't like someone else caring for

him, but he knew Ben was good with horses, so he agreed. "He's a little skittish around anyone else. I can brush him down when I get back."

Ben grinned. "Don't worry about this big guy. If he won't let me do more than get the saddle off, I'll let you know. Otherwise, I'll take care of him."

"Thanks, Ben." Clay patted Lucky. "You go on with Ben here, and I'll be back quick as I can to check on you."

Lucky sidestepped and whinnied when Ben led him away, but he settled down as the man talked to him and stroked his neck. Clay, relieved to know Lucky was in good hands, let Joanna help him to the buggy. Carrie stayed behind with the two small children. She and Hope stood in the yard waving as the others left.

Joanna sat in the backseat beside Clay on the way to town. Clay wanted to put his arm around her and hold her close, but he knew if he did he wouldn't be able to let her go. He couldn't think right now. His head hurt too much. He knew he didn't want Joanna to go through anything like what had just happened ever again. There might be other fellows bent on getting revenge. He didn't know. He couldn't remember. His past hadn't been a Sunday school picnic, though. Of that he was certain. A heavy weight of guilt and helplessness sat on his heart.

At Joanna's house, Clay climbed from the buggy feeling like a train had run over him. Sherman and Mariah went inside with them. Clay sat in the nearest chair while the others looked for Dr. Brady.

"Tom?" Sherman called to the empty house and received no answer.

Joanna went into the kitchen and came out carrying a slip of paper. "Here's the note I left telling him I would be gone. He hasn't been home."

"Maybe he was called out," Mariah suggested.

"No," Joanna shook her head. "He went to Mrs. James's house for dinner."

"Is that right?" Sherman grinned. "I saw them talking after church this morning. That wasn't the first time, either." He looked at his wife. "Didn't we see them together at the Fourth of July doings?"

Mariah smiled and nodded. "Ruth James is a wonderful woman, Joanna. Your father couldn't do better."

Joanna sighed. "I know. I don't have any objections, except I wish he'd get home and take a look at Clay." She walked over and touched Clay's forehead. "Are you all right?"

Her fingers felt cool and soft against his skin. He grinned at her, wishing he could keep her standing beside him, touching him. "I've been hurt worse and lived."

"Oh Clay, I'm so sorry."

"This wasn't your fault, Joanna." Clay leaned his head back against the chair and closed his eyes. Her hand dropped to her side. "I'm to blame for signing on with a bunch like that in the first place."

"Whoso keepeth the law is a wise son: but he that is a companion of riotous men shameth his father." Mariah's soft voice brought rebuke to Clay's heart.

He opened his eyes and looked at her. "That's from the Bible, isn't it?"

She nodded. "Yes, from Proverbs 28:7."

"I reckon I can be thankful my father doesn't know what

kind of man his son has become. He never stayed put in one place, but he was a law-abiding man."

Sherman pulled a straight-backed wooden chair close to Clay and straddled it facing him. "Clay, there isn't a one of us can claim that we've lived our whole lives without sin and be telling the truth."

Clay shrugged. "Maybe." He hesitated and then said, "I mean no disrespect, sir, but I've not lived a charmed life. I haven't had a home that I could remember. My companions, like Mrs. Butler said, were riotous men for sure. I don't think you realize just how far into sin I've gone."

Sherman chuckled. "At one time, Clay, I might have been one of those riotous men you've known if you'd lived in Texas about thirty years ago."

"You?" Clay stared at the gentleman rancher. Everyone knew Sherman Butler was an upright citizen, member of the church, and wealthy rancher.

"Yep, me." Sherman nodded. "Once, before I met the Lord, I had a pretty bad reputation in Texas as a gunfighter. I grew up in the North, and I hated Southerners because of what a couple of them did to my mother during the war. You see, the war didn't end for me in '65. I kept it alive with my riotous living. Then one day I met a Someone who took that hatred away. Jesus Christ gave His life for me. When I accepted His gift of salvation, He gave me a new life. Clay, He can do the same for you."

"I don't know." Clay looked at Joanna. She and Mariah sat across the room quietly listening. She gave him an encouraging smile.

At that moment the door opened and Dr. Brady walked in.

"Well, what have we here? A library committee or"—he took a second look at Clay—"or a head wound? Sherm, can you help me get the young man to my examining room?"

Clay pulled himself forward and stood with Sherman's help. "That's okay. I can walk."

As Dr. Brady cleaned and bandaged Clay's head, Sherman filled him in on the afternoon's events. The doctor mixed some white powder in a glass of water and handed it to Clay. "That should fix you up. Drink this, and it should knock away some of the pain. I want you to take a couple of days off work, and Sherm, have someone check on him through the first night. Wake him up about every two hours. He's got a concussion. Send someone for me if there's a problem."

❧

On Wednesday morning Joanna walked to the library. She'd spent the last two days doing nothing but thinking about Clay and reliving the horrible experience they'd gone through. Her father had seemed to understand her need to recover, and although he didn't say anything, she knew he worried about her and had been praying for her.

But this morning she decided she had to get on with her life. She couldn't hold on to what would never be while hiding away in her room until she grew old and slowly lost her mind.

She pushed the front door of the library open and went in. Wiping a trickle of perspiration from her face, she crossed the front room to the shelves Clay had installed for her. She ran her hands over the smooth wood and knew she would never forget him. As long as she had the position of librarian, she would have a bit of Clay with her in the work he had done.

She opened a box that had been dropped off and retrieved the top book. She might as well get to work stocking the shelves. She hadn't heard from Clay since Sunday, except her father said he was recovering nicely. She hurt even though she hadn't expected him to contact her. Not after what had happened. He probably wished he'd never asked her to marry him. Maybe it was best she had been unable to give him an answer.

Joanna had been working for an hour or so when the door opened and Carrie rushed inside. "Oh, Joanna, I'm so glad I've found you! I didn't know where else to look when you weren't home."

"What's wrong?" Joanna scrambled to stand from her sitting position on the floor. "Is it Clay? Did he take a turn for the worse? Can't you find my dad?"

"Whoa." Carrie held up both hands to stop Joanna's flow of questions. "Clay's fine. I just wanted to tell you he's leaving."

"Oh, is that all?" Joanna turned to straighten a book on the shelf. "I suppose we always knew he would. It's probably for the best anyway. He doesn't stay in one place long, you know."

Heavy footsteps on the porch caught their attention. Mark stepped through the open doorway. "Joanna, are you all right? I heard about what happened Sunday, and I've been wanting to come see you ever since but didn't know if I should. Then I saw you walk past the feed store a while ago and decided it would be okay. Everyone said you were all right, but I just wanted to see for myself that you aren't hurt."

Joanna forced a laugh. "I'm fine, Mark. Nothing happened really. Not to me anyway. They caught the men, so all is well."

"Oh, that's something else I wanted to tell you," Carrie

said. "Luke got word just this morning about those men. He held them overnight here and wired the U.S. marshall. They were charged with kidnapping and two counts of attempted murder plus a list of other crimes they've committed. Anyway, when the marshall was taking them to the county seat to be tried, Simms almost got away."

Joanna's eyes widened. She visualized the huge, filthy man who had held her prisoner, and her heart pounded. "He's free?"

"No, I'm sorry, Joanna. I didn't mean to scare you. He tried to get away from the marshall, but his hands were in cuffs behind his back and he couldn't control his horse. The horse fell in the chase, and Simms broke his neck. He died instantly."

"Oh, that's terrible." Joanna felt a rush of pity for the man who had probably never been taught right. "I mean, I'm glad he won't bother us anymore, but I didn't want him to die."

"I understand."

"Well, I don't." Mark frowned. "The guy deserved to die after what he did to you."

"I suppose," Joanna said. "But we all do wrong, Mark. I never expected anything like this to happen, but I've learned my lesson well. I'll be content with the life God gives me. And I'll be more careful whom I associate with from now on."

"Are you saying you've decided Shepherd isn't the man for you?" Mark asked.

A sad smile touched Joanna's lips. She shook her head. "I guess Clay never was for me. Carrie says he's leaving now anyway, so it doesn't matter. I've resigned myself to being an old maid librarian."

"Why don't you go tell him how you feel?"

Mark's question couldn't have surprised Joanna any more if he'd asked her to marry him after all she'd done to him. "What are you talking about, Mark?"

Mark shrugged. "Maybe I'm learning a little about romance now that I've found someone who really cares for me." He smiled. "I owe you, Joanna, for nudging me in the right direction. Now it's my turn. You love Clay. You always have. I saw him kiss you way back when we were kids. You remember. I can see it in your eyes. You never knew I was there because I didn't stay after what I saw. But I hated Clay after that. I was jealous. That's all."

"You aren't anymore, are you?" Joanna saw her answer in the contented expression on Mark's face before he answered.

He shook his head. "Nope. I love you, Joanna. Guess I always will, but now I know the difference between having a friend and having a woman to stay with for the rest of my life. I don't know what will happen with Liz, but I hope to give us a chance. I think you need to give Shepherd that same chance."

Mark took Joanna's hands in his and looked into her eyes with a slight smile. He leaned forward and kissed her cheek. "I wish you and Clay the best."

Joanna watched him leave through a sheen of tears. She turned to Carrie with a shaky smile as she wiped the moisture from her eyes with the tips of her fingers. "I've had a productive summer, haven't I? Here I am, twenty years old, and I have no prospects for marriage because I've run off two of the best men around."

Carrie gave Joanna a sympathetic hug before she stepped back and searched her face. "Tell me what's going on between you and Clay. You went on a special picnic Sunday afternoon, and now you aren't even speaking to each other. He's packing to leave, and you say good riddance."

Joanna felt silent tears run down her cheeks, but she ignored them. "I don't know what Clay's problem is. He asked me to marry him just before Simms stepped out from behind the tree. After that everything changed. He acts now as if he never proposed. At least that's the way he acted Sunday. I haven't seen him since."

"And what's your problem?"

Joanna sighed and blotted her face with her sleeve. "Clay isn't a Christian, Carrie. I can't marry someone who doesn't believe. I know he goes to church, but will he later? You know the Bible says we should not be unequally yoked together with unbelievers. I've struggled this summer in my faith because of Clay. I let him come first before God. I can't do that anymore."

"What if I told you that isn't an issue now?"

Joanna stared at Carrie. "What do you mean?"

"Last night Clay accepted Christ. My dad and Cyrus had a talk with him. They said he prayed through to salvation. Joanna, Clay still thinks his past is a problem. He thinks he isn't good enough for you because of the things he did before. That's why he's leaving. If you love him enough, you won't let him get away."

Joanna's surprise and delight brought a wide smile to her face. She swiped at a new source of tears and laughed. "I do love him."

"Then come on. I've got the buggy outside waiting."

"Can you take me by my house first? Will we have time?"

"Sure, if it's important." Carrie shoved Joanna out the door and closed it after them. "Let's hurry, though. He isn't leaving until after lunch, but he doesn't have that much to pack."

After a quick trip to the house, Joanna had what she needed to convince Clay she loved him. Carrie pushed the horse, and they covered the ground quickly. Joanna jumped from the buggy as soon as it came to a stop in the yard at the Circle C. Carrie told her to look in the middle bunkhouse where Clay stayed with three other hands, so she ran in that direction.

The door stood open and Joanna looked in. Clay stood with his back to her, stuffing a bag with clothing. Her heart sank. He really was leaving, and he wouldn't have told her. What if she couldn't convince him to stay?

She stepped into the long room that held four bunks. "Clay."

He stiffened and then slowly turned, the expression on his face cautious. "Joanna? What are you doing here?"

"I came to stop you from leaving." She took a step forward.

"I can't stay. You of all people should know that." He turned back to his bunk.

"Okay." Joanna felt her heart break. What more could she say? "If you have to leave, I'll try to understand, but I've brought you a going away gift."

"You didn't have to—" Clay stared at the dried mistletoe she held up.

She continued moving closer to him as she talked. "Do you recognize it, Clay? I was standing under this mistletoe seven years ago when you kissed me. I fell in love with you then. I haven't stopped loving you since."

Before she lost her nerve, Joanna lifted the mistletoe and held it over Clay's head. He didn't move as she stepped close enough to touch him. He didn't move when she touched her lips to his. He started to pull away as she wrapped her arms around his neck. Then with a sound deep in his throat, he crushed her to him and took control of their second kiss.

The love in his eyes when they pulled apart nearly took away what little breath Joanna had left. She smiled, and he smiled at her.

"I haven't forgotten that you asked me to marry you, Clay. I didn't get to answer Sunday, so now I'm saying yes. If you are leaving, you will have to take me and my mistletoe with you."

Clay grinned and took another kiss before he answered. "Are you sure you want to hook up with someone like me?"

Joanna nodded. "I'm not afraid of your past, if that's what's worrying you. Carrie told me you accepted the Lord. Don't you know He's able to take care of us just like He did Sunday?"

"Yeah, I guess that's right. He's already started working in my life. By the way, you aren't the only one who fell in love under that mistletoe. I love you, Joanna, with all my heart. So when can we get married?"

Joanna giggled. "Are you busy this afternoon?"

Clay grinned. "Sorry, I've got to get my job back. Let's take enough time to find a place to live and let you fix all the frills you want. How's that sound?"

"Perfect." Joanna couldn't say anything else as Clay claimed her lips once more.

epilogue

The trees lining Main Street had burst in autumn's brilliant colors of red, yellow, and orange before Joanna and Clay were married in the little church in Cedar Bend, Kansas.

Joanna stood beside her father at the back of the church, holding Hope's hand. As matron of honor, Mariah Butler followed the bridesmaid, Elizabeth Cramer, up the center aisle where they took their places to Pastor Carson's right.

Mariah had confided in Joanna just the day before that God was going to bless the Butlers with another little one. Only this one would come the conventional way. Next spring Mariah would give birth for the first time at the age of thirty-eight. Joanna breathed a prayer for her friend and the unborn baby.

She glanced at Carrie and Luke Nolan, sitting near the front with their baby son. He had been born only two weeks ago, and Joanna had been privileged to help with the delivery. Luke held Daniel, who at nine months of age tried to steal the show with his happy smiles and baby babbles.

Ruth James sat just behind the Nolans with her four children. Last week Joanna's father had asked her to be his wife, and she had accepted. He had teased Joanna, saying he had to have someone to cook for him now that she was leaving him. Joanna knew the truth. He had fallen in love with Ruth, and she was glad because Ruth seemed to be just as much in love.

Sherman Butler stood in front beside Clay. Next to Sherman, Mark Hopkins stood with a pleasant look on his face. He seemed to be watching the bridesmaid more than anyone else. Joanna didn't know the outcome of Mark's romance with Liz, but she expected a wedding would take place when school dismissed in the spring. Both Mark and Liz had been helpful in getting the library off to a good start, and they had become some of Clay and Joanna's closest friends.

Joanna released Hope's hand and bending low said, "Okay, now you can go. Do you remember what you are to do?"

The little girl looked up at Joanna with big brown eyes shining and lifted her basket. "I just got to throw these flowers on the ground."

Joanna smiled and gave Hope a gentle push forward. "That's right. And then go sit with Carrie and Luke in front."

"I know, Aunt Joanna. I'm a big girl." Hope stepped forward, taking a handful of flower petals then tossing them in front of her. She watched them settle to the floor before taking another long step and repeating the process.

By the time Hope reached the front, Joanna no longer watched her as her gaze moved to Clay. He smiled, and Joanna smiled in return.

"Are you ready for this?" Her father spoke beside her.

She turned to give him a brilliant smile. "Oh yes, Dad. This is the adventure I wanted all along."

"Then let's go."

As they stepped forward, Joanna watched Clay's smiling face and thanked God for giving her the desires of her heart and bringing her even closer to Him in the process. Maybe praying for an adventure hadn't been such a bad idea after all.

A Letter To Our Readers

Dear Reader:

In order that we might better contribute to your reading enjoyment, we would appreciate your taking a few minutes to respond to the following questions. We welcome your comments and read each form and letter we receive. When completed, please return to the following:

Fiction Editor
Heartsong Presents
PO Box 719
Uhrichsville, Ohio 44683

1. Did you enjoy reading *Joanna's Adventure* by M. J. Conner?
   ☐ Very much! I would like to see more books by this author!
   ☐ Moderately. I would have enjoyed it more if

   _____

   _____

   _____

2. Are you a member of **Heartsong Presents**? ☐ Yes ☐ No
   If no, where did you purchase this book? _____

   _____

3. How would you rate, on a scale from 1 (poor) to 5 (superior), the cover design? _____

4. On a scale from 1 (poor) to 10 (superior), please rate the following elements.

   ____ Heroine   ____ Plot
   ____ Hero   ____ Inspirational theme
   ____ Setting   ____ Secondary characters

5. These characters were special because? _____

_____

_____

6. How has this book inspired your life? _____

_____

_____

7. What settings would you like to see covered in future
Heartsong Presents books? _____

_____

_____

8. What are some inspirational themes you would like to see
treated in future books? _____

_____

_____

9. Would you be interested in reading other **Heartsong
Presents** titles? ❏ Yes ❏ No

10. Please check your age range:
    ❏ Under 18   ❏ 18-24
    ❏ 25-34   ❏ 35-45
    ❏ 46-55   ❏ Over 55

Name _____

Occupation _____

Address _____

City, State, Zip _____

Heartsong

Any 12 Heartsong Presents titles for only $27.00*

HISTORICAL ROMANCE IS CHEAPER BY THE DOZEN!

Buy any assortment of twelve *Heartsong Presents* titles and save 25% off of the already discounted price of $2.97 each!

*plus $3.00 shipping and handling per order and sales tax where applicable.
If outside the U.S. please call 740-922-7280 for shipping charges.

HEARTSONG PRESENTS TITLES AVAILABLE NOW:

Presents

Great Inspirational Romance at a Great Price!

Heartsong Presents books are inspirational romances in contemporary and historical settings, designed to give you an enjoyable, spirit-lifting reading experience. You can choose wonderfully written titles from some of today's best authors like Wanda E. Brunstetter, Mary Connealy, Susan Page Davis, Cathy Marie Hake, Joyce Livingston, and many others.

When ordering quantities less than twelve, above titles are $2.97 each.
Not all titles may be available at time of order.